The Gray Flannel Shroud

The Gray Flannel Shroud

by Henry Slesar

Random House   New York

To Œnone

Contents

The Gray Flannel Shroud

I. Eventually—Why Not Now?

It was his first morning on the Sword's Point railway platform, and Dave Robbins looked about him with interest. There were wintry, Wagnerian clouds overhead, and naked black trees undulated like musical notes over the suburban hills. It was a moody, mysterious morning, heavy with melancholy; there was something positively Russian about it. Dave checked *that* thought in a hurry, and looked at the men he would be sharing railway seats with on the ride into New York.

They weren't much different from the men he lunched with in east-of-Madison restaurants, competed with for taxis, huddled with in office elevators, joked with in agency meetings. But here, gathered like a silent regiment awaiting orders, surrounded by bleak hills and open sky, they seemed strangely transformed.

He looked at his watch. It was three minutes to the hour,

and the station platform was filling rapidly. There was polite jostling among the standees, a murmuring chorus of well-bred "pardon me's" as the crowd grew denser. Feeling himself an outsider, Dave gave in readily to the will of the throng, shifting his feet apologetically to the edge of the wooden platform. In the distance, a clacking sound became audible, and a pinpoint of light stabbed at the thick haze. "Excuse me, pardon," somebody said to him, and Dave moved again, his toes almost protruding over the edge.

The sound grew louder, a rhythmic succession of metallic snarls. Dave was suddenly uneasy. He held his overnight case close to his thighs, as if to form a wall between him and the onrushing train. There were other feet as close to the threat of iron wheels as his, but something told him to be afraid.

The something was right. It was as if a sudden convulsion took place in the midst of the crowd, an eruption of movement that overthrew the precarious balance of his position. He felt himself tottering, swaying; he threw back his elbows and tried to regain his footing. Then he knew the effort came too late, and he fell forward into the cinders.

The crowd gasped, but he felt rather than heard their startled reaction. For a single wild moment of hysterical fatalism, Dave Robbins thought he could only lie still across the ties and blackened cinders, waiting for crushing death. Then the sharp edge of the suitcase jabbed his stomach, and the pain brought sense to his actions. He leaped to his feet, flung himself back towards the platform, and a dozen outthrust hands pulled him to safety as the train roared in.

The commuters were solicitous. For a while, Dave was more than an outsider; he was a fellow human yanked back from the brink of eternity. Dave brushed at his overcoat, thankful for the thick padding that had kept him unhurt, and swung aboard with the rest.

He was an object of curious inspection on the trip, but he didn't mind. Then he began to suspect that it was more than the accident which was earning him the interest. He was sure they recognized him as an interloper, a weekend guest returning to his dingy, airless room in the city, where he really belonged. For one thing, he was hatless. For another, he wore his straight black hair long, abjuring the trim collegiate style. And just to make things worse, he was the only man on the train without a newspaper. He had a book, though, and for the first time he was grateful for it despite the title: *The First Age of Poetry*.

The book had been Janey's idea. Janey was an art director at Hagerty Tait Associates, and the fact that her last name was Hagerty had nothing to do with her ability. The first day that Dave Robbins spent at the advertising agency, he had noted the name on her door and raised a meaningful eyebrow. Six months later, he was convinced that he had been wrong to cry nepotism. The boss was Janey's uncle, all right, but the job had been earned by Janey's talented pencil. Six months after that, Dave was sharpening it for her.

There was only one thing wrong with Janey Hagerty. She was a culture buff. Dave looked at the book in his hand, glanced surreptitiously at the heavy-set man wheezing into the *New York Times* beside him, and began to read.

The history of Sanskrit literature is difficult to compose, due to the total lack of a fixed chronology. However, it may be readily divided into two periods, the Vedic and the Classical . . .

Dave thought of a dirty word. Then he sighed and turned back to the text. Eventually, on the third page, he discovered a poem. It had a lot of white space around it, and Dave, the advertising man, appreciated that. It was called "The Salutation of the Dawn."

> *Listen to the Exhortation of the Dawn!*
> *Look to this Day!*
> *For it is Life, the very Life of Life.*
> *In its brief course lie all the Verities*
> *And Realities of your Existence;*
> *The Bliss of Growth,*
> *The Glory of Action,*
> *The Splendor of Beauty.*
> *For Yesterday is but a Dream,*
> *And To-morrow is only a Vision;*
> *But To-day . . .*

Not bad, Dave thought, without conviction. He closed the book on his forefinger and gazed out of the window at the flashing scenery, the whitened countryside lying still and quiet under the season's first snow, the peaceful rise of smoke from the little houses along the route.

Look to this Day! Dave Robbins thought.

He shut the book and reached into his coat pocket for his Daily Reminder List, and traced a finger down his penciled notations.

Things to Do—January 3

1. *Must see Ross about Sugar Babies premium.*
   Sugg: plastic atom sub, called Nautilus?
2. *See Tait about trade ad for Cleveland Grocer.*

3. See Countess about TV participations in Cincinnati for Mother Maggie's Apple Pie.

4. Check strained prunes exploding on grocers' shelves.

5. Tell Janey loved her book.

At ten minutes to nine, the train screeched into Grand Central, and Dave allowed the milling crowd to convey him to the street. He reached the agency offices at nine, Dave's earliest hour of arrival since he had joined Hagerty Tait Associates almost eighteen months ago.

He had started as an assistant account executive to Gordon Tait, the executive V.P. and agency partner. It was a good deal for both of them. Dave was a new boy in the business, having had only a little more than a year of agency experience. Two wars and a laggard college education had made it hard to get a foothold, so he didn't mind being called "assistant" at the age of thirty-three. He handled all the details on the Burke Baby Foods account, the mainstay of the agency, and had full responsibility for the Baked Goods Division of the Burke Food Company. That left Tait with nothing to do but keep the Burke people happy and entertained. Dave used to gripe about that to Janey, until she pointed out that keeping Kermit Burke happy was a full-time job in itself.

When he stepped out of the elevator on the twelfth floor, he realized again how early he was. The only person in the lobby was Jody, the receptionist, and even she hadn't had time yet to settle down with her novel. She blinked at him in surprise and forgot to flash her professional smile.

"Well, we're *early* today," she said.

"Just a ghastly mistake. Am I the first?"

"No. Miss Hagerty's been in since eight." She was staring at his cinder-black overcoat. "Shall I order coffee for you, or will you wait?"

"Now," Dave said. He stood at the desk and looked around the lobby. The original idea of the décor had been Early American, until somebody had the notion of painting each wall a different, vivid color. On the red wall to the left, a bank of light boxes displayed the latest proofs of Hagerty Tait advertising. On the blue wall to the right, shadow boxes held dummy packages of the clients' products. On the yellow wall in the center hung a Gargantuan wagon-wheel clock, its wooden hands symmetrically pointing to nine.

Instead of going straight to his office, Dave walked down the corridor to the left and headed for the Art Department. The hallway was dark, but there were lights in the studio bullpen, and a soft glow behind Janey Hagerty's door. He knocked once and turned the knob.

"Ye gods," Janey said, looking up from her drawing board. "What brings *you* here in the middle of the night?"

"Passion," Dave said, shutting the door dramatically. "Quick, take off your clothes."

"Not before my coffee. Got a cigarette?"

He handed her one and she lit it coolly. Everything Janey did had a coolness about it. She was a pretty girl who could have been beautiful if she had valued beauty a little more. She cut her blond hair closely, almost mannishly, because of her distaste for curlers and permanents. There was a minimum of makeup on her sculptured face, with its delicate, milk-glass complexion, because makeup was so much trouble to apply. She wore "sensible" clothes. On a figure not as curvaceously compact as Janey's, they would have looked careless. On her, they looked fine.

"Tell you the truth," Dave said, "I've been roughing it for the weekend. Went to Sword's Point to see Bob Bernstein."

"Roughing is right. You look like you've been shoveling coal."

He told her about the accident, and liked the way it tenderized her eyes. But she got over the mood and said:

"How's Bernstein? Is he upset about losing the Burke job?"

"I guess so. He's been photographing the Burke ads since the agency got the account; can't understand why we've switched in the middle of the campaign. I couldn't tell him."

Janey looked thoughtful. "He's a good photographer. One of the best."

"Then what made them dump him?"

"I'm not sure. Maybe Uncle Homer was just tired of him. Or maybe Kermit Burke wanted a change. Who knows?"

"Well, it's a damn shame." He wandered to her bulletin board and looked at a tacked proof of a Burke Baby Food ad. "He took mighty fine pictures, if you ask me. You're the art director on the account; didn't they consult you?"

Janey didn't answer, and Dave suspected he had touched a sensitive area. He grinned and said:

"Say, that was a pretty good book you loaned me."

"*First Age of Poetry?* Glad you liked it."

"*This is the Salutation of the Dawn,*" Dave quoted. "Not bad at all."

"Oh, I dunno." She put the pencil to her mouth and

cocked her head at the layout on the pad. "I kind of like this line better. 'Grocers of Cleveland—Attention!'"

They laughed, and Dave said: "I'll need that little masterpiece this morning; Gordon wants to see it."

"He won't see it today. He'll be out. But you can relay any messages through Queen Tait; she's coming into the office this morning."

"Gordon's wife? What for?"

Janey shrugged. "Don't ask me why Queen Tait does anything. She called about an hour ago. The switchboard wasn't open, so I took it on the night line. Said something about Gordon not feeling well, but that she was taking the train in to see Uncle Homer."

"What's wrong with Gordon?"

"Virus or something. Queen Tait didn't deign to give me any details."

"Say, what have you got against Mrs. Tait?"

"Who, me? I love the dear woman. I keep her picture on my dresser; every morning I stick pins in it."

"Women," Dave sighed. "Well, I better beat it. Got a new idea for a Sugar Babies premium I want to talk to Harlow Ross about. A little plastic submarine called the *Nautilus*. You fill it with baking soda and it dives up and down."

"Brilliant," Janey said. "I've got an idea, too. How about a little vial of prussic acid? Be the First Kid on Your Block to Disfigure Mummy."

"Very funny."

"Oh, I've got loads of them. How about a kiddie-size prophylactic kit; an Educational Toy? Or one of those little miniature liquor bottles? Just like the one Daddy keeps under his pillow . . ."

"Goodbye," Dave said. "I can see you're in no mood to talk sense. So long, Charles Addams."

Dave went to his office. There was a stack of unopened mail on his secretary's desk, but he left it untouched. Louise was sensitive about her job, and if Dave took one privilege away from her, her eyes were red and wet for the rest of the day.

She arrived at twenty to ten, and was dismayed to find Dave sipping his morning coffee.

"Oh, I'm terribly sorry, Mr. Robbins," she said, her homely face already screwing up in preparation for tears. "I just couldn't get started this morning. It's my mother; she's practically helpless with arthritis, and I had to make breakfast this morning—"

"That's all right," Dave said uncomfortably. "Would you see if Mr. Ross is in yet? If so, ask him if I can drop by."

"Yes, of course," Louise said, trembling with the importance of her assignment. Dave frowned as she skittered out of the room. You'd think I'd asked her to find Garcia, he thought.

A few minutes later, she returned triumphantly. "He's in!" she announced.

Harlow Ross was sucking on his pipe when Dave came into his office down the hall. There wasn't anything unusual about that; Ross was always sucking on a pipe stem. He had half a dozen briars in his desk, and enough rough-cut tobacco for a parley of all the Indian Nations.

Ross was a slim man who looked taller than he was in his well-cut, narrow-fitting flannels. His hair was brush-cut and salted at the temples, adding the distinction of age to a youngish, handsome face, with prominent, heavy-lidded eyes. He looked like a romantic college professor, the kind who makes female students giggle in the back of classrooms. He was the account executive on the Sugar Babies cereal account, and he had been with Hagerty Tait since the agency doors opened for business.

"Morning," he said amiably, knocking his pipe noisily against the rim of an ashtray. "Heard you were out in my neck of the woods this weekend, Dave."

"Yep, went to see Bob Bernstein. He's got a nice little place, all right. But me, I'm still a city boy."

"You'll change your mind," Ross chuckled. "It's the wave of the future, Dave. Besides, you got half the agency out in Sword's Point: Hagerty, Gordon, me, even Kermit Burke. We could open a branch office."

"And commute from the city? It's a switch, anyway. Who was the joker who named the place?"

"I dunno. But I'll bet he was an ad man."

Ross laughed, yet the sound wasn't satisfying. There was a deliberate heartiness in everything Ross did; Dave thought of him as a professional nice-guy. Before his arrival on the scene, Ross, a widower, had been dating Janey Hagerty with some regularity. It was hard to like your girl's old flame, even if the ashes were supposedly cold.

"Say, Harlow," Dave said, "I've been thinking about that premium problem of yours. How about a miniature plastic sub, maybe called the *Nautilus*? You know the kind of thing I mean, works with baking soda."

"Been done," Ross said. "Think Kellogg did it a couple of years back. But I'll check into it, Dave."

"Okay, just thought I'd mention it." Ross' face didn't show much gratitude, and Dave shrugged. Then he recalled

Friday's luncheon encounter at LeVal's, and said: "Say, I meant to ask you, Harlow. Didn't I see you with that personnel guy from BBD&O last Friday? I was sitting a couple of tables away. Tried to eavesdrop, but I couldn't."

"Oh, that." Ross flushed slightly. "Just a friendly chat."

"You don't have to kid me, Harlow. You weren't thinking of making a switch, were you?"

"Of course not. But it never hurts to talk, you know that. Never know what will happen around here."

"As long as Burke is in the shop—"

"That's what I mean. Burke Foods spends seven million and our total billing is less than ten. You know what they say about eggs in the basket, Dave. If our eggs ever broke—"

"I wouldn't worry. Kermit Burke's nuts about this new campaign, and it's good for another three years. And the way Gordon handles the account—well, I wouldn't worry."

"Sure," Ross said, smiling pleasantly around the edges of his pipe. "Understand Gordon's sick today?"

"Virus," Dave answered.

At ten minutes to eleven, Dave stuffed an attaché case with the facts and figures on the Cincinnati trading area. Then he told Louise he would be out for the rest of the morning, calling on the Baked Goods Division of the Burke Food Company. Louise looked crushed by the information, but reluctantly accepted his call to duty.

He met Gordon's wife, Grace, in the lobby, waiting for the down elevator.

Grace Tait was a reedy, high-shouldered woman, cast in a *Vogue*-approved mold. Some years ago, she had decided that her motif was silver. There were silver streaks in her cocoa-brown hair, and silver highlights on her fingernails and eyelids. Her wrists jangled with silver ornaments, and there was a silvery edge in her carefully controlled voice. All in all, she had the esthetic appeal of a stack of fresh-minted coins, and from the little Dave knew about her, the analogy was more than apt.

"Morning, Mrs. Tait," he said. "Understand Gordon's under the weather."

"Yes." She whispered the word. "He—he asked me to bring something into the office for him."

"Well, you tell Gordon to take care of himself. He's the indispensable man around here."

They got into the elevator together, but the conversation had ended.

Dave hailed a cab in front of the building, and gave the driver the address of the Burke Baked Goods Division in Long Island City.

When they reached the block-long brick pile that housed the huge baking plant and executive offices of the company, Dave's stomach did its familiar loop-the-loop. The Countess Szylensca, President of the Burke Division, represented half a million dollars' worth of billing to Hagerty Tait, making it the agency's second largest account. More important, the Countess exerted an influence over Kermit Burke that involved the entire seven-million-dollar operation. Dave wasn't sure he was the man to handle the responsibility.

Homer Hagerty thought he was. He had thought that Dave's tall, thin figure, his slightly European features, his just-right age, would appeal to the Countess' taste in men. And that appeal (Homer Hagerty was a practical man) was more important to the security of the account than any advertising know-how.

The Countess Margaret Szylensca was the genuine article, an emigrant blue-blood who had come to America some twenty years ago with her titled husband. The Count had long since gone to his special corner of Heaven, but not before he had seen his beloved wife established in a properly American business enterprise. His original idea was to produce fine European baked goods, the stollen and strudel and delicate little kuchen that had once been lovingly prepared in the iron stoves on the ground floor of his ancestral home. But the Countess had become shrewder after his death, and set the sights of her lorgnette on the great American mass market. Her products became honest apple, cherry, blueberry, lemon, pineapple, and chocolate pies, little six-inch circles of pies whose wax wrappers bore a drawing of Mom, proudly displaying a smoking pie on a platter, and the brand name MOTHER MAGGIE. Count Szylensca wouldn't have approved of the pies, but he would have certainly been pleased with the bank balance of the company.

It had only been a year ago that Kermit Burke became interested in the Countess' little pies. The purchase of her company had been one of his pet projects, and he had handled the details himself. It had been hard for the Countess to relinquish sovereignty over her business, but she had seen the monetary advantages, and they were more important than pride. Besides, she still retained her title as president, and her authority as head of the Baked Goods Division.

Despite her willingness to cater to the great American market, the Countess still clung to some Old World sentiments. Gordon Tait had handled the account in the beginning, but she had accepted his services grudgingly. He was *too* American for her, too crew-cut, too hearty, too tweedy. But she approved highly of her new account executive, Dave Robbins. He was *her* kind of man: thinly aristocratic, dark-eyed and dark-haired, exceedingly polite, charmingly young, but not *too* young. He held her chair for her at meetings, lit her cigarettes, flattered her, noticed her new clothes or changes in her coiffure. The Countess, in official stories, described herself as forty-one. In private confidences she admitted to forty-eight. Actually, she was fifty-six.

Dave walked into the building, thinking rapidly of his opening statement. For two months now, he had been dodging a weekend invitation from the Countess, on one pretext or another. He was running out of pretexts, and the Countess was becoming increasingly annoyed at his refusals. He knew that the safety of the account was in the balance. Fifteen percent commission on half a million dollars was seventy-five thousand gross profit—seven times Dave's salary. And one little weekend could muck it all up.

Dave shrugged, and stepped into the sweet-smelling elevator on the ground floor. He punched the button marked four, and took a deep whiff of the rich bakery smell.

He remembered what the chief production man, Jorgenson, had told him, about why he had entered the business when he was a youth. Jorgenson had lived in Denmark as a boy, and being poor, had made nightly trips to the neighborhood bakery to purchase a great bagful of day-old baked goods for a few kroner. He had loved this warm, sweet smell so much that he had sworn to become a baker. Yet after a few years with the great ovens, he discovered that his nose had become immune to the wonderful odor, and all that was left was the heat and the hard work and the late hours. For some reason, the story made Dave sad.

He knew the Countess was in her office the moment he left the elevator. Jorgenson was just coming out, looking pale and shaken.

"Morning, Dave," he said gloomily. "One of her bad days. Hope you're taking your Miltown."

Dave grinned. It was Jorgenson's standard sally, and Dave always took it with a grin, despite the fact that it was uncomfortably true. About three months ago, Dave had taken some distressing symptoms, involving stomach pains and a fluttery heart, to a physician. An elaborate diagnosis had produced no evidence of organic disturbance, and Dave was forced to accept the idea that he was becoming prone to a fine case of Madison Avenue jitters. He resented the notion of being a pill-taker, but now there was a bottle of Meprobomate in his desk drawer, and he faithfully took a tranquilizing dose every afternoon.

"You ought to try it yourself," he told Jorgenson amiably. "Might help you stand the gaff."

"It's *her* needs the pills," Jorgenson said sourly.

Dave took a deep breath and turned the knob. As usual, it was a shock to find the equivalent of an eighteenth-century drawing room behind the businesslike façade. The Countess, seated behind a gold-embossed Napoleonic-era desk, her hair in a black turban, looked up with a frown when he entered.

"Ah, the genius," she said scornfully.

"Morning, Countess." He smiled brightly, and stepped across the deep-napped carpet to the coat closet. He hung his overcoat carefully and brought the attaché case to the desk. She watched him with glaring eyes, but Dave pretended not to notice.

"Got the stuff I told you about. Looks like a pretty good deal. These local cooking shows have a small but fanatically loyal audience. Now in Cincinnati—"

"David!"

He paused. "Yes, Countess?"

"Look at me."

He looked. She was a fairly striking woman, but not because of physical good looks. Time had taken that away. Her secret was color, and she used it dramatically to distract the eye from the lines in her face and the imperfections of her figure. The black turban was matched by a black dress. A string of coral beads wound four times about her neck. Her skin was stark white against scarlet lipstick and sea-blue eye shadow.

"You look very nice," Dave said.

"I don't ask for compliments, David. I wish only the truth. You told me last Friday you would have a great deal of work to do this weekend. Is that so?"

"Well, yes, I did say that."

"So of course, you could not accept my weekend invitation?"

Dave realized that the Countess knew more than he thought possible. He gave her the frank look.

"To tell you the truth, Countess, I *did* expect to be working. But things cleared up late Friday afternoon—"

"Never mind." She held up a ringed hand. "If you dislike the idea of a weekend in my company, David, simply say so. I won't trouble you with my invitations again."

"Now, Countess! Margaret—"

"Please. Go on with your business."

"But I *do* want your invitation. Really, I do. Look, how about this weekend? I'm sure I'll be free then."

"Yes. Until something better comes along."

"Countess, I *swear* to you—"

"Never mind; we'll talk of it later." She leaned back in her chair and gestured with the cigarette holder. "Now let us speak of Cincinnati . . ."

An hour after he returned to the office, Homer Hagerty's beautiful secretary Celia called Louise, Dave's secretary. Between them, they managed to convey the idea that Dave was wanted in the president's office.

Dave reached into his desk drawer for the bottle of Meprobomate before making the trip upstairs. He went to the water cooler and downed one of the small white pills. What with the incident on the railway platform, and the Countess' pique, he could afford to be tranquilized.

In front of the presidential office, Celia smiled warmly at Dave—more warmly than usual—and told him to go right in.

Hagerty's greeting was equally warm, and the president came around the desk to sit beside him on the sofa.

Homer Hagerty looked like any one of the two dozen white-haired character actors who were wise and witty in Hollywood movies. He was handsome, but with a kind of good looks that created paternal rather than romantic images. He had a voice that would have sounded fine from the pulpit of a fashionable church. Was he bright? Nobody ever asked the question.

"How long's it been?" Hagerty asked. "Two years, Dave?"

"Eighteen months. I started in July."

"Guess you know our operation pretty well then, eh?"

"I'm not sure I understand."

"Come on, boy, you're smart. You know this agency. We've got more than seventy-five percent of our billing in one account. It's a good account, true, but some people think that's a precarious way to exist."

Dave cleared his throat. "Well . . ."

"You don't have to say anything. Right to this minute, I'd say that Burke was the safest client in the business. This new campaign is the hottest thing they ever had. It's a little early to tell, but I got a tip-off from the Nielsen Survey boys that sales are already showing the effect. Don't let anybody ever tell you that it doesn't pay to advertise."

The academics of the discussion had Dave puzzled. He lifted an eyebrow and waited for the president to continue.

"So it's not the creative end we're concerned about," Hagerty said. "That's being handled beautifully. We're all proud of Joe Spiegel."

"He's a good man," Dave said.

"The best. A sweet guy, a great writer. As for Janey—" He frowned. "Well, you know how I feel about her. She's more like my daughter than my niece, Dave, but I'd fire her in a minute if I thought she couldn't do the job. But those Burke layouts are great, aren't they?"

"Sure are, Mr. Hagerty."

The boss smiled blankly. "You see a lot of Janey, don't you?"

"I guess so."

"Very practical girl. And brainy, too. Never could understand that. Her mother was a sweet woman, but no giant brain. As for her father—well, he was more like me, Dave. Beer and pretzels." He laughed pleasantly.

Dave tapped his foot. Hagerty had something on his mind, obviously, and it wasn't Janey's personality.

"Well, just wanted to tell you, Dave. We got a lot of regard for you here; you've done a great job. But now we've got a new problem . . ."

"What's that?"

Hagerty flipped open an inlaid box on his desk, but changed his mind about taking the cigar.

"It's Gordon," he sighed. "Had a heart attack last night, and a pretty bad one. We've sent the best heart man in New York to look him over, but from what I hear, things don't look too promising."

Dave swallowed hard. "You mean he's—"

"Dying? I didn't say that. Millions of men get heart attacks and live to write books about it. This was pretty severe, though, and it looks like Gordon will be out of action for quite a while."

"Gosh, that's too bad."

"Yes, it's bad," Hagerty said broodingly. "Sure sorry for old Gordon. He's only fifty-two, you know. But you can't push yourself the way Gordon does without paying the penalty . . ."

Dave waited for the important question. When Hagerty remained silent, he said:

"What's going to happen to Burke meanwhile?"

"Ah," Hagerty said. "Glad you mentioned it. As a matter of fact, Dave, I'm going to ask you to take over."

"Me?"

"Don't think it wasn't a hard decision to make, Dave.

Maybe you know that Harlow Ross has been lined up for Gordon's job since the day we started business. Harlow's a good man, very good. And a hell of a nice guy."

"Yes," Dave said, in a choked voice.

"But he's a little lightweight, to tell the truth. A little too Ivy League for Kermit Burke. You know how he is."

"I'm afraid I don't. I've never even met Burke."

"Well, he's a peculiar guy. I don't think Harlow would really *understand* him. I'd hate to take a chance like that right now."

Dave was shaking his head, almost involuntarily.

"No, Mr. Hagerty. I don't think so . . ."

"No, what?"

"I don't think I'm ready for Burke. Only three years in this business; that's not enough for an account like Burke."

"Dave, listen. Sooner or later, you'd have gotten your big break. Eventually—so why not now? There's another five grand in it."

"I'll have to think it over."

"Of course!" the president said heartily. "You think about it. You might even talk it over with Janey tonight. You *are* seeing Janey tonight?"

"Yes."

"Well, she's a clear-headed girl. Ask her opinion. If you decide anything tonight, you can even call me at home. Janey knows the number, of course."

"All right, Mr. Hagerty."

At ten o'clock that night, Janey leaned across the sofa in Dave's apartment and bit his ear. He said "Ouch!" and got his revenge. Then he stood up and went to the telephone. He dialed her uncle's number, and told him the decision. "Wonderful!" Hagerty said. "You'll never regret it, Dave." He was wrong.

II. Children Cry for It

Masters Pavilion boasted a façade of blue-tinted glass and artfully trimmed shrubbery, and might well have housed an avant-garde art museum instead of a hospital. Even the nurses seemed to have been chosen for decorative effect, and Dave Robbins looked upon them with appreciation. When he stepped into the quiet-running elevator that would take him to the third floor and the ailing Gordon Tait, he sniffed the air and realized that the usual carbolic smell of hospitals had been supplanted by Arpège and Chanel Number Five.

The perfume odor grew stronger as he swung open the slatted door of Room 311, but there was an obvious source. Grace Tait was at her husband's bedside, and where Grace walked, a cloud of Paris' sweet product was sure to follow.

Gordon Tait lifted his hand weakly from the bed sheet when Dave entered, in a gesture both gallant and cordial. Surprisingly, Dave wasn't shocked at the sight of the stricken executive. He'd expected to be jarred by the contrast, by seeing this robust, tweedy man, with his proud head and Johnny Walker stride, laid low by an insidious trick of the ventricles. But Gordon managed to look as hearty and cocksure as ever, and his pale, lined face might have been accounted for by nothing more serious than a vodka hangover. He grinned at Dave and, in his best Walter Pidgeon grunt, said:

"Ho, Athos! How fares the battle?"

"Same as ever." Dave smiled, and nodded courteously in the direction of Grace Tait. She returned the nod, but with a look that carried some indecipherable message.

"*Illegitimus non carborundum*," Gordon said. "Don't let the bastards grind you down. Say, you know my wife, don't you, Dave?"

"Yes, certainly."

"Well, what's the poop? I haven't heard any decent shop talk since they lowered the boom on me."

"Don't," Grace said crisply. "You know what Dr. Dishman said, Gordon. You're not supposed to worry about the office."

"Hell, who's worrying? Long as Dave's on the job, I can make a vacation out of this."

"Thanks," Dave said wryly. "I'll do what I can, Gordon, but I don't expect to fill your shoes."

Gordon Tait chuckled. "Just watch out for Kermit Burke in the clinches, Dave. Keep your left in his face. And if he ever gets really tough, come to papa. I've got a little dossier on Mr. Burke that'll come in handy."

Dave looked at the account man with admiration. He was only two days out of the oxygen tent that had been necessary to keep his heart pumping, and he seemed as much a part of his special world as if nothing had intervened. He was relaxed. It was as if he had an inside track on Destiny's ledger; he seemed to have a confidence in the future that Dave, too often a victim of the Fickle Finger, couldn't help envying.

He remained at Gordon's bedside for another half-hour, talking business. Then he left. But at the elevator door, he heard Grace Tait's voice at his ear.

"Mr. Robbins—"

"Yes, Mrs. Tait?"

"May I speak to you a moment? Before you go?"

"Sure." He looked around and spotted a door to a waiting room filled with low-slung furniture and subdued lamps. They went inside, and he offered the woman a cigarette.

She took a puff, stamped it out, and began to cry.

"I'm sorry," she said finally, not looking at him. "It's been a strain; I didn't mean to use your shoulder—"

"Perfectly okay."

"It's just that there's nobody I can talk to. Gordon has no family; mine's in California." She paused.

"He's terribly ill, Mr. Robbins. Much more than he thinks. And you know the way he is; even if Dr. Dishman told him—he'd just refuse to believe him."

"Gosh, I'm sorry," Dave said, sounding boyish. "Gordon's a fine man; I like him a hell of a lot. But from what I understand, millions of people get heart attacks and feel fine later. It's a sort of warning, the first time; if they take care of themselves—"

"It may be too late for that. Dr. Dishman—he's not too optimistic."

"That's a shame." She was looking him squarely in the face; Dave hoped his expression was sufficiently sympathetic. He was sincerely grieved by the woman's story, but he was even more uncomfortable.

"I'm just frantic about it. I don't know where to turn. If anything happened to Gordon—oh, I know it sounds terrible, Mr. Robbins, to talk about such things now. But Gordon doesn't even carry insurance. He—he never believed in it, never thought anything could happen to him."

Dave swallowed. "Well, there's the company insurance, of course. I'm sure Mr. Tait has the group plan; that's about thirty-five thousand."

"No, please." She touched his hand, and the silver jewelry was icy against his wrist. "Let's not talk about it any more. It's too terrible to talk about—"

"I'm sure he'll be all right," Dave said inanely.

"Yes, of course." She stood up, drying her eyes quickly with a crumpled bit of cambric. "I'm just overwrought; I didn't mean to burden you."

"I understand," Dave Robbins said. Awkwardly, he reached out and patted her hand. "I'm sure everything will be fine, Mrs. Tait."

There was a tear frozen on the woman's smooth cheek. It glinted silver in the light of the waiting-room lamps.

"Like all great ideas," Joe Spiegel said, "this one is simple."

Dave sat back in the plush conference-room chair generally reserved for agency clients, and watched Joe Spiegel, the agency's creative head, do his stuff. He was standing at the far end of the twelve-foot polished wood conference table, leaning on a wooden podium that held the mounted proofs of the new Burke Baby Food campaign.

Spiegel looked more like a country storekeeper than an advertising man. He was big-boned and virtually fleshless, and his rimless glasses kept sliding down to the end of his sharp nose. He had his coat off and his shirt sleeves rolled to the elbows, and displayed a pair of red galluses that would have done credit to a southern politician. When he spoke, the words came out dry as biscuits, but they usually made sense. The Burke campaign was his baby, as Gordon Tait said humorously, and he was as possessive about it as a mother lion.

The day after Dave Robbins accepted the new assignment, he'd asked Spiegel to give him a thorough briefing on the campaign that Kermit Burke was so fanatically endeared to. Dave had seen the ads around the agency, of course, and he'd read the memos that drifted around it, but he wanted to hear the story from the campaign's creator himself.

"Let's start with our product," Spiegel said. "Burke Baby Foods are manufactured in Ohio, by strict government-approved standards. The ingredients are grown at Burke's own farms or shipped in from various farming subcontractors in the vicinity. All foods are cooked under pressure in spotless kitchens, and every jar is hermetically sealed. They make every variety of strained baby foods, as well as junior foods and cereals. They're attractively packaged, and priced in line with competition. Now," Spiegel said, fixing Dave with a glittering eye, "why buy 'em?"

"Well, if they're as good as all that—why not?"

"Ah," Spiegel said. "The voice of innocence. The sad

truth is this, my friend. These same facts apply to virtually every branded baby food on the market today. If there are differences, they're minor—and so technical, nobody really cares. But here's another question for you. What does every mother want?"

Dave shrugged. "A wedding ring, I suppose."

"A healthy baby," Spiegel said. "A bouncing, bonny baby, bouncier and bonnier than Mrs. Jones' baby in the next perambulator. And that's what Burke is *really* selling. Not prunes. Not carrots. Not bananas. But a bigger and better baby for *you*."

"Hear, hear!"

"Now—there's nothing new to that story, either. Brand X and Brand Y have been screaming about healthy, happy babies for years. Thousands of healthy, happy babies have gurgled in advertisements for every brand on the supermarket shelf. But the truth is, Mrs. America isn't *really* interested in thousands of babies. She's interested in only *one* baby. Her own. Now take a look at Korea."

"Huh?"

"Korea. Remember those stories right after the war, about the millions of starving, homeless kids? Do you think Mrs. America shed tears over their plight? Don't answer too fast. Those tear ducts held up pretty well, whenever they talked about a *million* hungry babies. But when a local newspaper took charge of *one* Korean orphan, *one* little girl, the whole damn city busted out crying. She made the headlines for weeks. She got thousands of dollars in gifts and contributions. Because she was *one* kid. She had a name, and a personality, and you could *identify* with her problems. And that's the big secret of the Burke campaign."

Joe Spiegel lifted the first mounted proof onto the podium. It contained three photographs and captions. The main illustration depicted a young couple on a park bench, their heads close together. The girl was obviously pregnant. They had a shy, wonder-touched quality that was affecting. The headline read: "THEY'RE GOING TO HAVE A BABY."

"Here's the first ad of the series we call the Burke Baby," Spiegel said, "and it sets the pattern for the rest of the campaign. *One* young couple, Irma and Howard Clarke, about to face the greatest adventure of their lives—their first baby. *One* baby, mind you. Not even twins; we made sure of that. Our ads will show them planning, thinking, hoping—all for *one* baby. Will it be a girl or a boy? Who will it look like? Will it be blond, like Irma, or brunette, like Howard? What will they name it? Will they need a larger apartment or a bigger house? Will they have grandparent problems? And most important—will it be a bouncing, bonny, healthy baby? Think of the suspense!

"And as for the Sell, we look right down here in the copy and find out that the Clarkes plan to raise the infant *exclusively* on Burke Baby Foods. What will happen? Will Burke Baby Foods produce the kind of baby that puts Mrs. Jones' scrawny infant to shame? Watch this magazine next month—and find out!"

"A cliffhanger," Dave murmured.

"Exactly. And what do we see next month?"

Spiegel lifted up the second advertisement and placed it over the first. "THE BURKE BABY IS BORN" read the headline.

"Here we see the actual moment when mama meets papa in the hospital. Their baby has just been born, and it's a beautiful, seven-pound man child. They're going to call it

Donald, after the paternal grandfather, and they're as proud as a pair of parents can be. Can't you see the effect on the readers? They're just as happy for the Clarkes as the people who actually know them. They've *shared* the suspense, shared the experience, identified with it—and they'll continue to identify month after month, in Burke Baby Food ads."

Spiegel put up the third ad.

" 'THE BURKE BABY IS ONE MONTH OLD.' And look at little Donald, being burped by his father. A heart-tugger if you ever saw one. And sure enough, we read that little Donald is *already* starting his Burke Baby Food diet. Now here's the fourth ad. 'THE BURKE BABY IS TWO MONTHS OLD!' Look at those rosy cheeks. How that kid loves his Burke Strained Prunes, his Burke Strained Bananas, and so forth! You can see he's going to be a real prizewinner already. Is that demonstration in print, or isn't it?

"Now let's skip a couple of ads and look at the rough layouts for the future. 'THE BURKE BABY HAS TEETH!' What a moment for everybody! 'THE BURKE BABY WALKS!' And here's one we run about a year and a half later. 'THE BURKE BABY TALKS!' I tell you, Dave, not even Garbo got the publicity little Donald will when he says his first dirty word."

Spiegel sat down, as if suddenly wearied.

Dave didn't say anything for a moment, but then he grinned. "It's even better than I thought it was, Joe. No wonder everyone's nuts about it."

"Thanks," Spiegel said sourly. "If you like it, send money."

"I like it, all right. How far along are we on the campaign?"

"Well, the fifth ad is in proof form already. That's the one that says 'THE BURKE BABY IS THREE MONTHS OLD.' We're just putting the next ad together down in the studio, but the 'four months' ad is still only in layout form. Gordon Tait was supposed to go up to the Clarkes' place with the photographer tomorrow."

"How about Janey? Doesn't she go with him?"

"Nope. Gordon never believed in letting the art director go to a shooting. Or maybe he didn't like taking Janey; figured that Bryn Mawr wife of his would scream adultery."

"Well, I'll take Janey," Dave said, firm-jawed. "How about approvals? Kermit Burke seen this new layout and copy?"

"Nope. I think Gordon meant to take it down today. Guess that's another errand you'll have to perform."

"I guess so."

"Ever meet Kermit Burke?" Spiegel asked, pushing his glasses to the bridge of his nose.

"No. Have you?"

"Just once, but it'll hold me."

"What's he like?"

Spiegel grinned. "You better judge for yourself."

At two-thirty, Homer Hagerty stuck his silvery head into Dave's office and smiled benignly. He was wearing his camel's-hair coat and winding a Black Watch plaid scarf around his neck. "All set?" he said.

"In a minute. Got to pick up the layout from Traffic. Nice of you to come with me, Mr. Hagerty."

"Glad to do it. Seems only right that I introduce you to Kermit myself. I'm sure you two will get along fine."

They watched the mailroom chief wrap the package. Dave said, in a voice deliberately casual: "Understand that Bob Bernstein isn't shooting the pictures any more."

Hagerty didn't react beyond a shrug.

"He's a pretty nice guy, I thought; spent the weekend with him. But he's not sure why he got canned. Anything I should know about?"

"Nothing very important. He just rubbed some people the wrong way, that's all. But we've got an excellent replacement for him, man named Smalley. Hurry up, hurry up!" Hagerty said, suddenly scowling.

In the elevator, the long, flat package beneath his arm, Dave asked: "What kind of guy is Burke?"

"Nice, very nice. Kermit is real folks, Dave, you'll like him. Runs the biggest business of its kind in the country, but he never lost the common touch. Not *too* common, of course."

On the street, hallooing for a taxi, Hagerty added: "He knows what he wants, though, you've got to give him credit for that. He may talk like a hick sometimes, but Kermit is shrewd. If he drops a little hint, or makes a suggestion, don't pass it off lightly, Dave. It's an order."

In the lobby of the Burke building, Hagerty took off his homburg and wiped the sweat from the inner band. "When he's *really* friendly, Dave, that's the time to watch out. Then you know he's getting ready to slip the needle in. You got to be on your toes every minute, or you're a gone goose." He frowned angrily.

"Nice guy, very nice," Dave said sourly.

"That's the trouble with this lousy business." Hagerty scowled. "It's got too many clients in it."

They walked across twenty yards of green carpeting to get to the double doors that opened on the executive offices of Burke Baby Products, Inc. The receptionist, encamped behind a desk that outspanned Homer Hagerty's, nodded pleasantly to the agency head and looked at Dave suspiciously. Hagerty spoke to her for a moment, and she picked up the telephone.

A few minutes later, what was obviously a deposed Hollywood starlet came out of a side door and walked towards them with the studied languor of a Ziegfeld Girl going down the stairs. She flashed a high-candle-power smile, tilted her hip, and guided them through a corridor. From Hagerty's greeting, Dave surmised that she was Kermit Burke's secretary.

The hallway was lined with past and present examples of Burke Baby Food advertising, beginning with a sickening opus, circa 1931, headlined "What does a baby dream of?" Each exhibit was framed with the care of a museum masterpiece.

Finally, they were in the Presence.

Homer Hagerty plunged across the depths of the carpet that covered the massive, square office, his arm outstretched. Kermit Burke was ready to take it, and he pumped it up and down with the delight of an old friend at a reunion.

"Hiya, Cubby!" Hagerty said. "Nice to see you again!"

"Nice seein' *you*, Home Run!" Burke grinned back.

For a moment, Dave wasn't sure he was hearing right. He stood behind the boss, shifting uncomfortably on the unstable nap of the carpet. Then Hagerty turned to him, almost as an afterthought, and said:

"Cubby, want you to meet one of my best boys, Dave

Robbins. He's going to take over until Gordon gets back on his feet. Dave, shake hands with Kermit Burke."

Dave extended his hand gingerly. But when Burke met it, his handshake was limp and distinctly cool.

"Nice meeting you," Burke said casually. "Well, let's sit down, fellas. Got lots of chairs around here, might's well get some use outa them."

Hagerty laughed, and they pulled two chairs up towards the desk. Burke remained standing when they sat, and from Dave's viewpoint, he towered like some kind of rural giant over the desk. Kermit Burke was ungainly tall, with huge, floppy hands that rested knuckles-down on the desk blotter. His shaggy, wheat-brown hair was brushed forward on his sharp frontal bones, ending in a Napoleonic point. He wasn't young in the face, but his eyes went quizzical and boyish as he looked at them, and his wide mouth was puckish.

Finally, he sat down and reached into a desk drawer for a tobacco jar. He took off the heavy porcelain lid and lifted out exactly the right smoking implement, a corncob.

"Well, Home Run," he said, puffing and grinning at the same time. "Looks like we kinda run Gordon ragged. Hate to think I had anything to do with that."

"Of course not," Hagerty said heartily. "Never can tell about the heart. Could happen to anybody."

"Not to me," Burke frowned. "Not me, fella. Sound as a dollar. Smokin's the only vice I got, and my gramps smoked a pipe until he was ninety-seven."

He peered at Dave suddenly. "Well, young fella?"

"Pardon?"

"Waitin' for you to say something. That Gordon, he talked all the time. You going to be the quiet type?"

Dave smiled. "I'll talk when there's something to say, Mr. Burke."

"Mr. Burke?" The client looked mock-horrified and dropped a wink in Hagerty's direction. "You hear that, Home Run? I've made two bits off your boy already."

Hagerty laughed. "That's right, Dave. Forgot to warn you. Every time we call Cubby Mr. Burke, we got to put a quarter in the kitty."

"You said it," Burke said, pulling a baked enamel kitten bank out of his drawer. "Drop it right there, boy, and from now on, you call me Cubby. That's my nickname. What's yours?"

"Don't have one. My name's David."

"Okay, Davy Crockett, you can't throw me. Been hearing good things about you from the Countess—"

Dave gulped. "Glad to hear it."

"Fine woman, the Countess. Real quality, you know what I mean? And she thinks you're a crackerjack, Davey."

Hagerty said: "Dave's been with us two years now, Cubby, and he's been handling a lot of the detail work on your baby foods, too. So he knows a lot about the problems."

"Good," Burke nodded. "And what's your opinion of the baby campaign?"

"He thinks it's great," Hagerty said emphatically. "We were talking about it on the way down, and—"

"I'm askin' the boy," Burke said, suddenly with ice over his eyes. "Let's hear your absolute honest objective opinion of the Burke campaign."

Dave paused.

"I think it's great."

Hagerty sighed deeply and said: "We *all* love it, Cubby, you know that. It's the hottest property in the business."

"Got the new ad?" Burke said.

"Right here, Mr. Burke."

"Two bits! Two bits!" Burke chortled, and Dave grimaced and dropped another quarter into the bank. Then he unwrapped the package and showed the layout for Ad Six in the Burke Baby Food schedule. The headline was "THE BURKE BABY IS FOUR MONTHS OLD" and the main illustration showed the Burke Baby, young Donald Clarke, creating a rather shaky skyscraper out of alphabet blocks.

Burke stared at it for a long time, scrutinizing the suggested photos, reading and rereading the body copy. His lips moved as he read.

He looked up from the ad without raising his head, and a grin spread across his wide mouth. "Like it," he said softly. "Like it a lot."

Dave found himself sighing with relief.

"Got one little suggestion," Burke continued. "Little, little one. Don't have to bother with it if you don't want to. Won't make or break the ad, you know. Want to hear it?"

"Sure."

"See the alphabet blocks?"

"Yes."

"See what they spell out? Cflkpt. Makes no sense."

"Well, they weren't intended to *say* anything—"

"No, of course not. But they *could* spell out something, couldn't they? Like Burke's, for instance?" His grin widened as he peeked at Hagerty beneath the wheat-brown eyebrows.

"Wonderful!" the boss said. "Just the touch it needs!"

"Well . . ." Dave said.

"Now be honest," Kermit Burke told him. "If you don't think it's a good idea, you say so. Shucks, I'm a baby-food farmer, Davey, I don't know anything about advertising. Is it a good idea, or is it a bad idea?"

"I was just wondering, Mr. Burke. Would it detract from the believability of the photo? You know, the best part of this campaign has been the utter credibility of the pictures. Of course, the parents might have set the blocks up as a gag. That implication would be all right—"

"Well, you think it over," Burke said generously. "When you go down to the Clarkes' house tomorrow to take them pictures, why, you see if it doesn't work out. If it looks phony, you just forget about it. All right?"

"Sure," Dave said.

They were about to leave ten minutes later, when Kermit Burke stopped them.

"Oh, no you don't!" he chuckled. "Don't think I missed that last 'Mr. Burke,' Davey. I heard it all right! Pay up!"

Dave blinked at him, and shoved his hand into his pocket. He forced a wry grin, and plunked another quarter into the fat little kitten on Kermit "Cubby" Burke's desk.

When he returned to the office, Dave stopped at Janey's drawing board and told her the news about Burke's approval.

"Think we better shoot the main pic two ways," he said. "One with the blocks spelling out Burke's. Maybe I can convince him that his idea's off-base."

"Fat chance," Janey said. "The guy doesn't usually mess around with the layouts, but when he does—that's it."

"Well, we'll see. What time do we leave tomorrow?"

"Early, around nine. Have to be out at the Clarkes' house before it's time for little Donald's nap, and it's a good three-quarter-hour drive out to Willisport. That's where they live. The photographer will meet us out there."

"But you've never been there?"

"Nope. Your predecessor didn't think it was necessary. Afraid dear old Grace wouldn't like the idea of his traipsing around with a *femme fatale*. That's me, of course."

Dave grinned. "I like the idea. We can make an outing of it."

"What did you think of Kermit?"

"Old Cubby? Why, he's the nicest l'il ol' man I ever saw. Only got one vice, smokin' a corncob, and his gramps smoked one until the age of eighteen, when it killed him." Dave chewed an imaginary chaw of tobacco and spat it towards Janey's brush pot.

"Uncle Homer says he's smart."

"I don't doubt it for a minute. Also rich. He managed to get seventy-five cents from me in about fifteen minutes. Well, I better put the ad into the works. See you later, Daisy Mae."

On his office desk, there was a message scrawled in Louise's shaky handwriting. It had the desperate look of a suicide note, but all it said was:

"COUNTESS CALLED. CALL BACK."

Dave sighed, and asked the operator for Mother Maggie's number. She made the connection, and the Countess Szylensca said:

"Ah, David. How are you today?"

Her voice was sunny. Obviously, good relations had been

restored. Instead of making Dave feel better, it had him worried about how much better the relations would have to get.

"Just fine, Countess. Have you decided about the Cincinnati participation? We should buy in early—"

"Yes, yes, we'll talk about it," the Countess said impatiently. "But what I wanted to ask you doesn't concern Cincinnati. It concerns Romanvilla. You told me yesterday that this weekend would be all right. Is it still all right?"

"This weekend?" Dave said. The pain must have been evident in his voice, because the Countess' next words were frosty.

"You're busy, of course."

"No, no, it's not that. It's just that I've sort of taken on a new assignment here at the agency, and it might be difficult to—"

"I understand."

"No, listen, I'm sure I can make it," Dave said hastily. "Don't blame me for hesitating, Countess."

"Wonderful!" she said. "You will *adore* Romanvilla, David. It's like something transplanted from the Continent."

"I'm sure I will," Dave said, beating his head silently with a closed fist. "Now about Cincinnati—"

She laughed. "Please. Let's not speak of Cincinnati today. Cincinnati sounds like beer and sauerbraten. I feel too French today, David. We'll speak of it this weekend, if we get the chance."

"Fine," Dave said. "Goodbye, Countess." He hung up gloomily. "If we get the chance," he said aloud.

"What's that?" Louise said, entering the office.

"Nothing. Listen, Louise, can you order the company car

for tomorrow morning? To leave at nine promptly. We're going out to Willisport to shoot the pictures for the next Burke ad."

"Yes, sir," Louise said. "Oh, how I'd love to come with you, Mr. Robbins. That baby is just *adorable*." She hugged her steno pad and pencil against the flat plane of her chest, the eternal light of motherhood in her eyes.

"Smart, too," Dave said. "You know that he can spell out the name Burke's, with alphabet blocks?"

"Really? Why, he must be a *prodigy!*"

"Must be indeed," Dave murmured.

The morning sun washed into Dave Robbins' two-room East Side apartment the next day, and just in time to obliterate a nightmare. He forgot its scenario the moment he started brushing his teeth, but he remembered that two of its featured players were the Countess with a corncob between her teeth and Kermit Burke with a black turban around his head.

The company car, a somber Cadillac, was parked outside the building when he arrived at nine-twenty. Janey was waiting for him at the elevators, wearing a black coat over a simple tweed suit, and a frown on her milk-glass face. She took his elbow and wheeled him into the down car, saying: "We're late, friend. Don't forget baby's nap."

In the back of the car, as she looked at the red neck of Barney, the driver, the frown left Janey's face and she snuggled up.

"This is nice. All business should be conducted in the back seat of Cadillacs."

"My mother told me about girls like you," Dave said.

"What did she say?"

"She said she hoped I found one."

In another half-hour, Barney pulled up a side road and began a twisting route that led them to Willisport, some ten miles north of White Plains. It was a small, cozy town, whose roads were checked by radar.

They pulled the Cadillac alongside a parked station wagon in front of 321 Boxwood Avenue. A short, plump man stepped out to greet them. He wore thick-lensed glasses, and a hound's-tooth jacket that had no relation to anything else he wore. The leather case swinging from his shoulder and the Rollei in his right hand left no doubt that he was the photographer.

"Hi, men," he grinned, two teeth protruding. "My name's Ray Smalley."

"Darn," Janey said. "Knew I shouldn't have worn a suit. How do you do, Mr. Smalley. I'm really a girl, but I dress this way to discourage mashers."

Smalley's tiny eyes scanned her ripe curves appreciatively. "Say, you *are* a girl," he giggled. "I wouldn't mind a mash or two myself."

"I'm Dave Robbins," Dave said, not warmly. "You know what this assignment's all about?"

"Sure, pal."

"Have you seen the layout?" Janey asked.

"I know what's wanted. Say, I've been shooting babies since I could trip a shutter." He was still looking at her, and the leer was pronounced. "I could give you a little sample, honey. Any time you want to try out my bearskin rug—"

"Let's get started," Dave said gruffly.

He went to the door of the Clarkes' modest, two-story

home. There was still a Christmas wreath on the door, looking brown and ragged. He pumped the knocker twice, and the door was opened.

"Oh," the man said. "You must be from the agency."

"That's right," Dave smiled. "My name's Dave Robbins."

"Come in."

It was hot in the little house. The man who was obviously Howard Clarke took their coats and hats and stacked them, not too neatly, in the closet. He was an earnest-looking, youngish man. He wore a blue knitted pullover that was too long for him, and he kept rubbing his palms over the wool at his hips.

"The baby's in the playroom," he said, talking rapidly. "My wife's upstairs, putting on her makeup. We didn't finish breakfast too long ago; maybe you'd like a cup of coffee."

"I'd like that fine," Janey said.

"All right, I'll get some. Why don't you get comfortable, in here?"

The living room was dominated by an artificial-looking terra-cotta fireplace. The furnishings were roughly colonial, arranged formally around an enormous, varicolored hooked rug. They sat on the slatted wood-framed sofa, and Janey said: "Shame, Dave. You didn't even introduce us."

"Didn't have the chance. Awfully jumpy fella, don't you think?"

Smalley dropped his leather case on the floor and started pulling out film. He distributed his paraphernalia carelessly on the rug and said: "Well, where's little Ronald or Donald or whatever the hell he's called?"

"Shush," Janey said, and smiled up at Howard Clarke, entering with a tray that held three brimming cups. "Thanks,

Mr. Clarke. I'm Janey Hagerty, the art director on the Burke account. And this is Mr. Smalley; he'll be taking the pictures from now on."

"Oh?" Clarke said distantly. "Where's Mr. Bernstein?"

"He's not working for us any more," Dave said. "But I'm sure you'll find Mr. Smalley very experienced."

"Yes," Clarke said vaguely, looking towards the stairway. "My wife will be down any minute. Maybe you'd like to see the baby?"

"Love to," Janey said.

They went into the next room, a sort of combination dining and play area. There was a playpen in the corner, and a blond-headed little boy was poking his finger into the eye of a stuffed koala bear. He looked up when they entered, and his small mouth quivered uncertainly. He was a good-sized kid; he looked older than his four months.

"Isn't he *lovely?*" Janey squealed, bending over and touching his curls. "Just look at those *huge* eyes. Much prettier than his pictures. Doesn't he remind you of somebody, Dave?"

"I dunno. Winston Churchill?"

"Oh, don't be silly. Some movie star or other; something about the eyes and the mouth. I just can't place it . . ." The baby cooed at her, and Janey sighed rapturously.

Dave looked at his watch. "Almost ten-thirty. Could you see if your wife's ready, Mr. Clarke?"

"Yes, certainly," the man said, his hands pulling at his sweater. "I'll get her right down. I'll go upstairs and fetch her."

He backed out of the room. They heard his muffled footsteps hurrying up the carpeted stairs to the second floor.

"Something's wrong," Janey said.

"What?"

"Can't you see? He's *much* too nervous. I think something's wrong between him and his wife."

"Happens in the best of families," Smalley said.

"Well, why did it have to happen today?" Dave clucked. "We've got to make 'em look happy. After all, they're the parents of the *Burke* baby. They ought to be happy as kings."

They returned to the living room, and stared into the flameless fireplace. Smalley wandered about the place, prying into cupboards, examining the bric-a-brac on the shelves. Ten minutes passed, but there was nothing but the placid sounds of Donald in his playpen, and the ticking of the ormolu clock on the Clarke mantel.

"What the hell," Dave said. "What's the matter with these people?"

He stood up impatiently and went to the foot of the stairs. "Mr. Clarke?" he called.

No answer. He stepped up three of the stairs and called out again. Finally, he completed the trip up the stairway and stood at the door of their bedroom.

He was about to knock, when the sounds inside tempted him to eavesdrop. They were the sounds a woman made when she was crying. Dave put his ear against the door.

"I can't!" the woman's voice said. "I can't, Howie!"

"You've *got* to," Clarke's voice said tensely. "Those people are waiting, Irma. We've *got* to go down."

"I can't go through with it! Not right now. Tell them to come back!"

"No, Irma. You know what Mr. Tait said. We have to

go through with it, or you know what they'll do. We *have* to. For Donald's sake!"

There was a silence, and then Irma Clarke said: "All right. All right, Howie. Just give me another minute. Just one more minute. Please!"

Dave whirled and hurried down the padded steps.

Janey looked up. "Well?"

"They're coming down now," he said.

"Anything the matter?"

"No, nothing." He looked at Smalley, who was fingering a painted vase on an end table. "For God's sake, Smalley, stop poking around! This isn't your house."

The photographer looked surprised at his outburst, but put down the vase. A few minutes later, Irma and Howard Clarke came down the steps, smiling. There was a lot of white face powder around the woman's eyes.

They had dinner in town, and he tried to talk Janey into dropping up for a nightcap. She pleaded fatigue, and he walked her home. At the corner, he gallantly offered to buy her evening newspaper.

It was smack in the middle of an embrace on her doorstep that Janey said, "Oh my God!" and brought the front page closer to the hallway light.

"What is it?" Dave said, peering over her shoulder.

Her finger stabbed at a brief item at the bottom of the page.

"Bob Bernstein!"

He took the paper from her, and felt sick when he read the details of the photographer's sudden and unexpected death. An accident in the darkroom, the paper said. The account was terse, but the picture it created in Dave's mind was vivid. A jar of acid, Bob Bernstein's friendly, homely face . . . He shut his eyes.

"Poor old Bob," he whispered.

III. Ask the Man Who Owns One

The shock of Bernstein's death was still apparent on Dave's face when he reported for work on Thursday morning. Their friendship had been a brief one, but Bob Bernstein had been a warm enough man to make even a short friendship burn brightly.

He wondered if he should call Bernstein's wife and give his condolences, but he had only met her this past weekend. He hated the idea, and rationalized himself out of the duty. Instead, he busied himself in preparation for the job that had been handed him.

At ten o'clock, he asked Louise to get him Gordon Tait's files on the Burke account. When they came into his hands, he slipped out the one marked CONFIDENTIAL and began to read the accumulation of documents.

They were far from sensational. Most of them consisted

of letters to and from Kermit Burke, but it was obvious why they had been contained in confidence.

He picked up a typical communication and read it, noting that it had been written by Burke to Gordon Tait almost a year ago, before the birth of the Burke Baby campaign.

Dear Gordy:

I've finally had a chance to review the proposed campaigns you left in my office last week, and I'm writing to express my opinion of them.

Now you know I'm just a baby-food farmer, Gordy, and I never pretended to be an advertising genius. But my gramps used to tell me that common sense would carry me further in this world than anything else, and I ain't done so bad just by using my noodle.

Now, about those campaigns. Well, they sure had purty pictures. You ought to be real proud of the artist. The words weren't so bad, either, but I suspect they could have been more natural-like. Stuff like "vitamin-packed goodness" kind of throws me.

However, I have to admit that the ads impressed me over-all about like a skinny chicken—all squawk and no meat. There ain't an "idee" as my gramps would say, in the whole durn bunch. Looks to me like somebody in that fancy office of yours said: "Well, old Cubby Burke is flapping his lips again, fellas, let's get out the old ad-making machine. Let's make some purty pictures and write a lot of sappy things like 'vitamin-packed goodness' and he'll be happy. After all, he's only a baby-food farmer, what does he know about advertising?"

Well, Gordy, I don't know much, but my common sense

tells me that you boys are slipping on the mill wheel. If you spent a little more time thinking and a little less drinking, as gramps says, maybe us farmers would get more for our advertising dollars. After all, fifteen percent is fifteen percent.

So what can I do but bundle up the stuff and send it back? Maybe you fellas can come up with a real brainstorm in the next few days. I'll be mighty happy to see that happen. I got a lot of respect for you boys, and old Home Run Hagerty has been a friend of mine for years. But business is business, as the fella says, and a lot of pretty good agencies have been hammering on my door for a long time. Maybe the time's ripe to give 'em a chance.

Well, Gordy, the ball's in your court. By the way, I sure enjoyed meeting your lovely wife, Grace, last night. Maybe we can get together at my place sometime, if things work out right. Best wishes,

Cubby

There were other equally unpleasant letters in the file, but there were also several that indicated Burke's happiness with the new campaign the agency finally developed. One of the letters was from Gordon to Kermit Burke, and it read:

Dear Cubby:

I'm happy to say that things are really rolling now. We've scheduled the first shooting of the Clarkes for tomorrow morning, and have lined up Robert Bernstein, a top-notch photographer, for the assignment.

As you know, we planned originally to have two young couples involved—the Clarkes and the Addisons—just in case we ran into trouble with either birth. I regret to say that

Mrs. Addison's baby was born prematurely yesterday, so that automatically rules them out. The baby, being a six-month child, has been incubated; we don't believe the Burke Baby should begin life weighing only five pounds.

However, we feel confident that the Clarke baby will be just what we're looking for. As you can see by the Plans Book, we won't actually place the ads until three months after the birth, thereby assuring us additional protection.

Now about the changes you wanted in the copy. We feel that the phrase "vitamin-packed goodness" . . .

Dave skimmed through the other letters, noting the improved tone of Burke's messages. Obviously, old Cubby was delighted with his new campaign, and Dave had to admit that he was willing to give the agency full credit.

At the bottom of the letters file, there was a sheaf of financial reports concerning the Burke account. Dave was never much on figures, and he looked through these only cursorily, but the size of one of them stopped him.

A.G. $125,000.00

Dave was puzzled by the initials. He checked the media list, and found that they couldn't signify the name of any publication on the schedule. He went through the financial statements more carefully, trying to locate the initials again. They appeared nowhere else.

He picked up the phone and called Elaine, Gordon Tait's secretary.

"A.G.?" she said. "I'm sorry, Mr. Robbins. It doesn't mean anything to me."

"You sure about that? It's a hell of a lot of money. Maybe Gordon had some kind of private code."

"I don't think so," she said haughtily. "If he did, Mr. Tait would have told me about it. He told me everything."

"No doubt. Well, thanks anyway, Elaine."

He hung up and drummed his fingers on the desk blotter. It was a hell of a lot of money, all right, and there should be some accounting for it. The word reminded him of Sheplow, the agency treasurer. Dave made the trip to his office.

Sheplow was bent over a stack of bills, his eyes appraising them from behind the cleanest, shiniest pair of glasses in the world, a façade so brilliant that you were never aware of the soft brown eyes behind them. When he talked, his false teeth clicked like a comptometer.

He greeted Dave suspiciously. Sheplow treated all callers suspiciously. Like many treasurers, he identified personally with the agency's bank balance, and any incursions upon it, in the form of salary increases, advances, expense accounts, or even supper money wounded him deeply.

At his question, Sheplow snapped: "Of course I know about the money. I don't see why it's a concern of yours."

"Well, maybe Mr. Hagerty didn't tell you, but since Gordon's illness, I've taken over the Burke account. If the money's charged to my client, I'd like to know why."

"Charged to Burke? Nonsense. It's strictly an agency expense."

"Then why was the figure among Gordon's Burke papers?"

"Don't know, don't care. Mr. Hagerty himself authorized the withdrawal of that amount. It's charged against Hagerty Tait and not any individual client. I assume Mr. Hagerty had good reason."

Dave frowned.

"Do you know what A.G. stands for?"

"I do not."

"And I don't suppose you'd tell me if you did?"

Sheplow smiled thinly. "That's quite possible."

"Then I can assume it was some kind of personal withdrawal made by Mr. Hagerty?"

"Assume what you wish. Now if you'll excuse me—" He adjusted his brilliant eyeglasses and swiveled the chair around. Dave stood up, unsatisfied with the explanation, and yet unable to ask any more sensible questions. All he could do now was leave. He did just that.

He returned to his office and completed the examination of the file. Nothing else excited his interest, but the initials A.G. remained on his mind for the rest of the morning. Obviously, the man who could explain them was Homer Hagerty, but Dave was reluctant to ask the president. His next best thought was to ask the president's niece.

They had lunch at a small Italian restaurant off Third Avenue, a quiet homey place where the floors were badly slanted and the tablecloths suspiciously gray. But the food was good, and Janey liked it.

He asked his question over the espresso.

"A.G.?" Janey knit her milk-glass brow. "No, I can't imagine what it means."

"I found the figure among Gordon's papers, but Sheplow claims that your uncle authorized the withdrawal from the agency's bank balance."

"So?"

"You can't blame me for being curious. A hundred and twenty-five thousand is a lot of dough. Would you have any idea why he would withdraw such an amount?"

"No. Why should I? It must have something to do with the business. Maybe a tax deduction or something; I never could understand those things."

Dave looked worried when he lifted the hot, bitter coffee to his lips. Janey must have caught the look, because she said: "What are you getting at, Dave? Why all the fuss?"

"Well, I'm not sharp on finances, either. But I got the distinct impression that it was a personal withdrawal. Do you think your uncle might be in some kind of trouble?"

She answered quickly. "Of course not!"

"What makes you so sure?"

"Because I know he isn't. I know my uncle as well as I know anyone. If he was up to something crooked—"

"I didn't say that."

"Well, you *looked* it." Her cool countenance was suddenly warmer. "Uncle Homer and Gordon Tait are the sole stockholders. They can do anything they please with the money."

"Don't get so worked up. I didn't say he was juggling the books or anything. But you'll have to admit—there's something odd about a deduction that size."

"Only if you have a suspicious mind!"

They sat in glum silence for a while, and Dave signaled for a refill on the coffee, even though he hated it. He gave her a reconciliatory grin, and put his hand over hers. She jerked it away.

"Oh, come on, Janey. I know you're fond of the old guy. But you'll have to remember—he's just my employer."

"He's the finest man I've ever known," Janey said quietly. "You have no idea how wonderful he's been to me, Dave. I know you see him differently, but it's true. He's been wonderful to me and Aunt Clothie."

"You never talk much about your aunt."

"They've been married almost thirty-five years, and he still treats her like a bride. If you could only *see* them together. She's been an invalid for the past five years, and he almost never comes home without some little present."

"You make me feel like a rat," Dave said, arching an eyebrow. "Hell, I'm not knocking your uncle, Janey. I've got plenty to thank him for."

"Lots of people do," Janey said, not quite so stiffly. This time, when Dave's hand touched hers, she let it stay there.

At the office, Dave went looking for Homer Hagerty. But he paused in the anteroom when he saw that there was an altercation in progress at Celia's desk.

"I'm sorry," the president's secretary was saying. "Mr. Hagerty just isn't available this afternoon. I'll be glad to take a message."

"Don't give me that!" The woman who was leaning over her desk looked angry. She spoke in such menacing tones that Dave decided to continue eavesdropping.

She was wearing a shaggy coat of some indefinable but expensive fur, and it was exactly the wrong color for the violent, silver-blond hair that was piled high on her head. There was a small beaded bag in her hand, and pseudo-gold initials (or were they real gold?) gleamed under the reception-room lights. She was unusually tall, and had the stance of a showgirl, carrying her hairdo as if performing a balancing act. When she turned her head, Dave saw that she was surprisingly young, her face thickly coated with theatrical, phosphorescent makeup, her mouth redder than necessary. She had the striking kind of beauty that was popular on

Fifty-seventh Street placards, and from the ripple of her body beneath the fur, her figure was probably voluptuous to match.

"Don't give me that," she repeated. "He knew damn well I was coming up here today. Let me use that telephone a minute."

Celia flushed. "He's *not* in, though. He had to go to the hospital this afternoon. If you'd let me take a message—"

"I got a message all right. But you look like too nice a girl to hear it. Do you have his home telephone number?"

"No," Celia lied.

The woman smiled tightly, as if recognizing the loyal little falsehood. "Okay, sweetie, you've got your problems. But then I've got mine. So you tell Mr. Hagerty that he can call *me*."

"Certainly. If you'll give me your name and number—"

"The name is Gander. Miss Gander. And I think Mr. Hagerty *knows* the number."

Celia scrawled on a pad, and the young woman looked at the floral display on her desk. She smiled again, dazzlingly, and clipped a carnation from the stem. She dropped it into her beaded bag and snapped it shut with a distorted air of triumph. Then she turned and walked to the elevators, her heels clicking loud and hard against the floor.

Dave came up to the desk when she had gone, and said: "Whew! You get all kinds, huh?"

Celia said: "I suppose so." Then she got terribly busy.

Dave went down the corridors to his office, speculating about the nature of Miss Gander's vociferous interest in Homer Hagerty.

He was just about to sit down at his desk when he realized what the golden initials were that gleamed on Miss Gander's beaded handbag.

A.G.

He whistled to himself, and then decided to talk things over with Janey.

He found her deep in concentration over a series of small photographs, a dozen to a page. She was using a magnifying glass to study them, and frowning in the process.

"Hi," Dave said. "Those the culls from yesterday's shooting?"

"Yes. I've been looking at them all afternoon."

"Well, if you can spare a minute, there's something I wanted to ask you—"

She looked up blankly. "Can it wait? I've got a little problem."

"Sure. What kind of problem?"

"Maybe you can figure it out. But here's a batch of photos Bernstein took last month, for the Burke Baby ad. And here's the culls Smalley delivered this afternoon. See something odd?"

Dave compared them. "Not particularly."

"Don't you see something crazy?"

"I don't get you."

"About Donald, I mean. Don't you notice a difference?"

"Well, he's a month older, of course. Kids grow fast at that age."

She put her fingers through her hair.

"I guess you're right; I was just being silly."

"What was bothering you?"

"I'm not sure. But for a minute—I didn't think it was the same baby."

In his own office, Dave absent-mindedly reached for the bottle of Meprobomate and dutifully took his pill. He must have let it linger too long on his tongue before swallowing; the tranquilizer tasted bitter.

It was four-thirty, and he didn't feel much like working until quitting time. He thought of going back to Janey's office and studying the strange disparity she saw in the photographs, but a sudden spell of fatigue came over him. He leaned back in the swivel chair and looked out the window at the small piece of skyline that was admitted to his view. The air was growing hazy with the approach of darkness, and the metal peaks of the building were dimming. He rubbed his eyes and then his stomach, at the onset of a gnawing pain. Maybe the doctor was wrong about him, he thought. Maybe he *was* working up an ulcer after all . . .

The pain became more intense and he forced himself out of the chair, and went towards the water cooler. His foot couldn't seem to find the pedal that would start the spray, and he had to lean on the cooler for support when dizziness overcame him. What the hell, he thought.

Louise passed by and said something solicitous. He didn't hear her, but said something about being all right. Then he tried to return to his office. The doorway was at a peculiar slant, and he tried to right it with his hands. But there wasn't any strength in his fingers, and his stomach was increasingly unstable. He gave the whole thing up as a bad job, and, sighing, sat down on the floor and vomited. He was still sitting there when they came to help him, but he didn't know who they were.

IV. 99 and 44/100ths Percent Pure

He was on somebody's sofa, and there was a debate raging over his head. It was an academic debate, consisting mostly of amateur diagnoses and suggested remedies and indecision about what to do next. He thought he heard Janey's voice knifing through the discussion, and knew that what she must have been saying was sensible and right, and he hoped she would prevail. He didn't know if that was how it turned out; the next thing he was aware of was a moon-faced man with a squiggly mustache that ran beneath his nose like a penmanship exercise. Then there was the cold touch of a stethoscope's nozzle on his bare chest, and then he was giving mumbled answers to soft-spoken, pointed questions, and then he was sleeping and dreaming and feeling well, almost giddy.

He remembered something about a taxicab ride, too, and the sweet softness of Janey's hand on his face, and the cool sheet of his own bed that somehow felt more comfortable, more luxurious, than he had ever known it before. He remembered his face in the pillow, his ear cocked, listening to the pleasant sounds of kitchen activity, and he smiled to himself, envisioning Janey, calico-pretty, cheeks flushed from oven heat, stirring something in a bowl and humming to herself, the perfect picture of domestic loveliness. Then she was passing his bed, and he was reaching out for the silken leg flashing by . . .

"Ouch!" He opened one eye and rubbed his smarting wrist. "What'd you do that for?"

"Hands to yourself, mister. You're too sick for that kind of thing."

Dave tried to sit up, but didn't quite make it. "Who's sick?" he groaned sickly. "I'm not sick. I'm dying."

She sat on the edge of the mattress, her face concerned. "You feel worse?"

"Terrible. Think end is near. Better grant one last request. Ouch!"

"I said," Janey said grimly, "that you should behave yourself. If you ask me, the whole thing was a big act. I knew it was all a seduction routine."

Dave opened the other eye. "What the hell happened, anyway? I feel like my stomach's been scraped."

"You passed out at the office. We called a doctor in the building and he said it might have been some kind of food poisoning. But whatever it was, you got rid of it. The hard way."

"Food poisoning?" Dave's eyebrows twisted. "We both ate the same thing at lunch, didn't we? We had the scampi and the veal scallopini, both of us. Why didn't *you* get sick?"

"Thanks for the good wishes."

"No, seriously." He forced himself to sit up, and then noticed his pajamaed frame. "Hey, how did this happen?"

Janey's milk-glass cheeks reddened. "I found them in a drawer. You should tell your laundry not to put starch in your pajamas. They practically walked out of the bureau and got into bed."

"Gee, I guess we'll have to get married now," Dave said wistfully. "I've been compromised."

"Don't worry; I was a student nurse in college. That gives me special privileges." She wouldn't meet his eyes for a moment. When she did, she saw that the joking mood had left his expression. "What's the matter?"

"It wasn't food poisoning, Janey. Not that kind of poisoning. The last thing I remember before getting sick was taking a Meprobomate—"

"A what?"

"Miltown." Dave frowned. "I've been taking them for the last couple of months. No cracks, please."

"Miltown? But can it make you sick like that?"

"No. But I remembered this one tasting funny. Sort of bitter. I didn't think anything about it when I swallowed it, but I got the whimwhams a minute later. That must have been the culprit."

"You mean the pill was bad?"

"Could be. Maybe the formulation was off, or something. Or maybe—" He stopped.

"Maybe what, Dave?"

"You'll say I'm nuts. I know you will. But maybe it was something like arsenic, or cyanide, one of those. I mean maybe it was poison, pure poison."

"What an awful thought! How could poison get into your pill bottle?"

"I can only think of one way. Somebody put it there."

He dropped back to the mattress and shut his eyes, not even curious to see what jumbled emotions his words must have brought to Janey's face. Whatever sedative the doctor had given him was still effective, and sleep returned quickly. He had one brief, alarming dream before morning, involving an onrushing railroad train. Harlow Ross was in the engineer's cabin, a smelly briar in his mouth, black smoke streaming from the bowl.

He slept until ten-thirty the next morning, and woke up feeling surprisingly normal. He telephoned the office, and the switchboard operator, recognizing his voice, asked after his health.

"I'm fine, Mrs. Kennedy; I think I'll be in this afternoon. May I have Louise, please?"

She rattled off a home remedy involving camphor oil and a warm sock, and then got him his secretary's extension.

"Mr. Robbins' office," Louise said. When she heard Dave's voice, she began to sob.

"It's all right, Louise, I'm perfectly okay. It was just a little stomach trouble. Were there any messages today?"

"Only Countess Szylensca. I told her you were sick and probably wouldn't be in today. It was funny—"

"What was?"

"The way she sounded. She sounded as if she didn't believe me."

Dave groaned. "Okay, Louise," he said miserably. "I changed my mind about coming in. If anybody wants me for anything, I'll be home until about six. After that I won't be available."

He hung up, and dialed the number of the Burke Baked Goods Division.

"Countess? This is David."

"Oh, yes," she said icily. "I understand you're—not feeling well, David."

"No, no, I feel fine. Just a little stomach upset yesterday, but I'm fine now. I just wanted to let you know that I'm still set for the weekend, if you are."

Her voice brightened. "Oh? Are you certain, David?"

"Sure, positively. Might do me good to get away."

"You poor boy," the Countess said, all the iciness replaced by liquid, motherly warmth. "We'll take *very* good care of you at Romanvilla. You know, to be perfectly frank, when I called your office—" She laughed. "I thought you were merely creating another excuse for not coming to see me. That shows you what a silly woman you're dealing with."

"Don't worry. I wouldn't miss the weekend for anything."

"Good. I'll pick you up around six, David. Don't fuss with too many clothes; we're terribly informal at Romanvilla."

"See you at six, Countess."

He hung up, making faces at the telephone.

At noon, he got out of bed and made himself a breakfast-lunch combination consisting of scrambled eggs and a peanut-butter sandwich. The eggs tasted like brown velvet and the sandwich like plastic wood. At four-thirty, he started to get ready for the weekend.

"What's the matter with you?" he told his image in the bathroom mirror. "She's not *that* bad. And besides, she's a real, honest-to-God countess. How many chances does a guy *get* to sleep with royalty?"

The argument didn't satisfy him. The Countess Margaret Szylensca, for all her colorful plumage and title, simply didn't inspire him that way. And besides, there was Janey.

He groaned when he thought of Janey. She knew that the weekend was taking him off some place, but he had neglected to name his hostess. If she knew what he was about to do in the name of duty . . .

He buried the thought in a wet washcloth.

At five past six, he heard the sound of a multithroated auto horn on the street, and looked out the window. The car was big and red and Italian, looking brash and out of place among the parked Plymouths and Chevys on the street. He grabbed his suitcase and went downstairs to greet his hostess.

Fur was the keynote of the Countess' costume that evening. She wore a bulky mink that didn't suit her plumpish figure, a large fur hat decorated with tiny ermine tails. There were ermine cuffs on her black gloves, and Dave fully expected to see her drawing smoke from a fur-lined cigarette holder. She pulled back her lips in a canine smile when he entered the car, and greeted him in a pleased, furry voice.

"This is delightful, David. I do hope you're feeling well enough for the trip—"

"No question about it," Dave said. "It was just one of those things."

"I hear it was most distressing. Someone told me you actually fainted. Is that true?"

"Well, in a way. The way I figure it, it was some bad seafood. You know what that can do to you."

"Yes," the Countess said. "You must be very careful, David."

"Yes," he agreed thoughtfully. "I intend to be *very* careful, Countess."

The drive took over an hour, and it was far from comfortable. The Countess opened the side window, enjoying the rush of cold air on her face, bundling herself into the pile of fur. Dave was just plain cold in his unlined topcoat, but he'd be damned if he'd admit it. She chatted almost girlishly for most of the journey, except when they turned off on the expressway. Then she devoted all her energy to the wheel, pushing the foreign car to the limits of its considerable horsepower. She seemed awfully eager to get home, and Dave didn't like her anxiety.

When the trip was over, Dave's eyes were smarting from the cold and the wind, and he could barely discern the outlines of the big house that came in sight just off Peconic Bay. It was definitely Gothic, stone-vaulted and arched, and practically church-like in its vertical lines and high-rising steeples.

It was a relief to get indoors, where the ribbed vaults and flying buttresses and narrow windows were tempered by the more conventional furnishings: carpets from Gulistan, bric-a-brac from Jensen's, and furniture from Dunbar. There were more hallways in the house than there were rooms in most houses, and the living room (she corrected him by calling it the salon) was large enough to stage football practice.

A servant took their wraps, and they were finally settled, ice-cold martinis in hand, before an enormous stone fireplace, and the Countess herself made it her privilege to light the taper that set the great logs blazing. Dave had to admit that it was an extraordinary setting, but he didn't enjoy the feeling of being a young innocent about to be seduced by a female Dracula.

"There, now," the Countess sighed, leaning back into the corner of a curved, ten-foot sofa. "Not so bad, eh?"

"It's wonderful," Dave said grudgingly.

"Wait till you see it in daylight. The grounds are simply stunning. I used to do a great deal of work in the garden myself, but no longer. Are you *sure* you're comfortable?"

"Positive," Dave said, from the other end of the sofa.

"You're much too far away. Come." She patted the place beside her. "Sit here and talk to me. But not about business; you must promise that."

He came over, but couldn't make talk. Then the portrait over the mantel gave him inspiration. It was the picture of a grave, weak-chinned man in a blue epauleted uniform. He said:

"Tell me something about your husband."

"Andrew? What is there to tell? Andrew was simply Andrew. A gentleman of a school which no longer has its graduates." She laughed softly. "We were terribly young when we were married, betrothed by our parents when I was merely ten and Andrew fourteen. Imagine! That is one of the things I admire in America. Romantic love. Not always practical, perhaps, but rather fun. Don't you think?"

"Yes," Dave said. "Sure."

"Not that I wasn't romantic about Andrew. He was terribly handsome in his uniform. Were you in service, Dave?"

"Twice. They caught me a couple of times. But I doubt if I cut such a fine figure. I was a corporal both times. We don't wear epaulets, us corporals."

"Sit a little closer."

Dave inched over.

"I wish it would rain!" the Countess said dramatically, tossing back her head. "I love the sound of rain on these funny old windows!"

"I know what you mean," Dave said uneasily.

"There's nothing so snug, is there? Rain outside, fire inside . . ."

What the hell, Dave thought. It was unavoidable, inescapable. She couldn't have made the situation clearer by sending out engraved invitations. It was no good fighting for his honor any more; he was tired of pushing off the inevitable. He edged even closer to the Countess, his left arm slipping around her shoulder. Then he shrugged in a small gesture of surrender, and drew his right arm about her waist. She looked bewildered for a moment, and he kissed her.

"David!"

She didn't speak the name softly, lovingly. It was an exclamation of surprise.

"For heaven's sake, David! What are you doing?"

"Why, I'm sorry, Countess—"

"You foolish child! What do you mean by kissing an old woman *that* way?"

"What?"

She laughed explosively. "And right here, beneath Andrew's portrait! I'm afraid this is *too* much atmosphere for you, David."

"I don't understand—"

"Nor do I. But it's a pretty compliment, and I thank you for it." She looked at him with amusement. "Did you think I was leading you on? How terrible of you!"

"Now, look, Countess—"

"David, I know myself fairly well. I'm a silly woman about many things, but no longer silly, thank God, about men. If you promise not to repeat it, I'll tell you my *real* age. I'm forty-eight, David. I'm sure your own mother is about the same age. Now," she said, smoothing her skirts, her eyes still twinkling, "let's not say anything more about it. Besides, there's someone I wish you to meet."

"You mean someone else has been invited?"

"Not exactly. Someone else lives here." She smiled at him again, a smile of tolerant chastisement. "Now sit here, naughty boy, and I'll be back in a moment."

She left the room and Dave sat on the sofa, feeling like an idiot. He looked up at the portrait, and Andrew's face didn't appear so grave any more.

When the Countess returned, she was trailed by a young woman.

"David," she said, "this is my daughter Sonya."

She pushed the girl in front of her, and Dave blinked. She was a tall, ethereal figure with the paleness of her skin vividly contrasted by the corona of black hair that surrounded her head. She was thin-faced, with delicate bones that showed their fine tracery beneath her translucent skin. Her eyes were large and lavender, but their striking color was constantly concealed by a frequent lowering of her lashes. She was altogether as beautiful and unearthly a creature as Dave had ever seen.

"I—I didn't know you had a daughter," Dave said inanely, trying to smile.

"Few people do. But Sonya is the one thing I love best in all this world. Say hello to the gentleman, Sonya."

"Hello," Sonya said, in a soft, throaty voice. She extended her hand and Dave took it cautiously, wary of breakage. But the delicate fingers felt surprisingly strong. "Mother's spoken of you often, Mr. Robbins. I'm happy to meet you."

"But so *formal!*" the Countess laughed. "Come, let's all sit down. David, perhaps you can mix Sonya a drink; she likes old-fashioneds. Can you make one?"

"Sure," Dave said nervously. "Lead me to it."

"Over here," the Countess said gaily. "We'll have a lovely evening together. As a matter of fact, I have a wonderful idea for after dinner. We'll all play Scrabble!"

"That's fine," Dave croaked, picking up the whisky decanter. "Scrabble's just fine."

The firelight danced over the flying buttresses, and mother and daughter Szylensca sat on the sofa and watched in admiration as their guest prepared the drink with clumsy fingers.

Dave Robbins left Romanvilla at four that Sunday afternoon, and he was more than glad to take the train back into the city. It had been a totally different weekend from the one he had anticipated, but he wondered if the original wouldn't have been preferable. Because now he realized that the Countess' interest in him was still abiding—not as a lover, perhaps, but most definitely as a son-in-law.

It wasn't that Sonya was undesirable. There was an old-country magic about the girl, and a kind of misty beauty that Dave associated with faded royal portraits of queens and princesses. But Dave was his own man; he didn't like his affairs, love or business, arranged for him. It was with unconcealed relief that he returned to the harsh realities of the Long Island Railroad.

On the platform, he bought a newspaper and went inside the cramped station house to keep warm. The trains ran hours apart at this time of day, and it was a long wait. He settled down on a wooden bench and unfolded the paper.

He found the item boxed on page one.

WOMAN SLAIN IN
FIFTH AVENUE HOTEL

New York, Jan. 9. A beautiful young fashion model was shot to death early today in the Park Carlton Hotel on lower Fifth Avenue. The woman, Miss Annie Gander, was discovered at two-thirty p.m. by the hotel maid. The police . . .

Dave didn't read the rest, not just then.

He was thinking about golden initials on a beaded bag. A.G.

V. Accept No Substitutes

The man at the Cromwell Analytical Laboratories on Forty-eighth Street didn't look surprised or even greatly interested at the project Dave had in mind. He accepted the bottle of Meprobomate, with its remaining eight tablets, tagged it, receipted it, and promised to call Dave when the analysis was complete.

At the office, he had a difficult time getting the week started. There were too many interruptions all morning, from the employees of Hagerty Tait, who dropped into his office to inquire curiously about his health, and from his own troubled thoughts. It wasn't easy to concentrate upon advertising problems—not when he might be facing a problem of pure survival.

Had the pill bottle been tampered with? He asked himself the question without wanting to know the answer. Who would be sore enough at Dave Robbins (such a sweet, good-natured guy!) to actually want him dead? But then there was the railroad incident; was that more than an accident? Was Harlow Ross more deeply wounded by his promotion than he realized? Harlow lived at Sword's Point, but then so did a dozen other people in the company, from Hagerty on down. Or was it all mixed up with the mysterious Miss A.G., and the hundred and twenty-five grand deduction, and the dead woman in the fashionable East Side hotel . . . ?

Tune in tomorrow, Dave thought grimly, and find out. Or would tomorrow be too late?

"Monday morning blues?"

Joe Spiegel's nasal accents came from the doorway. Dave forced himself to grin companionably as the copy chief ambled into his office and jackknifed his long body into a chair.

Then Dave had an idea.

"Say, Joe, you have any police connections in this town?"

"Who, me? Not unless you count Traffic Court."

"I wanted some information about something. I called the *Times-Express* this morning, but I drew a blank."

"Who'd you call?"

"I dunno. City desk, I guess it was. All they could tell me was that the story was complete as printed."

"What story's that?"

Dave hesitated. Then he appraised Joe's open, bucolic face, and said: "Well, it's a murder story, matter of fact. Some woman killed in a hotel. The name sounded familiar, and I was wondering if it was somebody I knew."

"Tell you what," Spiegel drawled. "Why not use some of that Madison Avenue power?"

"How do you mean?"

"Call the advertising department. Hagerty Tait places a

lot of linage in the *Times-Express*. They'll be nice to you."

Dave looked puzzled. "What's the ad department got to do with it?"

"You *are* a new boy. Listen, just get the name of the *Times-Express* space rep from Media. Give him a buzz, tell him who you are, and ask for a chat with their crime reporter."

"That," Dave said, "is an idea."

"Ideas," Joe Spiegel said, "are my business."

The space rep's name was Gallagher, and he was delighted to be of service. When he called Dave back that afternoon, he said:

"Mr. Robbins? Your man's name is Max Theringer; he's the one who covered the Gander story. He's a pretty busy guy, but he can be free for an hour at five. Suppose you meet him at the City Room?"

"You mean at the newspaper?"

Gallagher chuckled. "Not quite. It's a bar across the street. And listen, don't mind the way he talks. Max is an old-timer, and he thinks the ad department eats babies."

"I understand. Art versus Commerce; the eternal struggle."

"How's that?"

"Never mind. Thanks a lot, Mr. Gallagher."

At three-thirty, the man from Cromwell Laboratories rang Dave's phone. The news was disappointing, but not unexpected. The bottle of Meprobomate contained eight Meprobomate pills. Nothing else.

At four forty-five, he took a taxi to the door of the City Room Bar and Restaurant, just below Forty-first Street. It

was a sour-smelling tavern antiqued with grimy wood panel-
ing and ground-in sawdust, catering exclusively, it appeared,
to men. Personally, Dave preferred soft lighting, foam rub-
ber lounges, and the punctuation of a female giggle in his
barrooms. But when he met Max Theringer in a rear booth,
he could see that the newsman was one of the breed that
clung tightly to this beery discomfort as being symbolic of
their hard-bitten profession.

"Mr. Theringer? I'm Dave Robbins." He stuck out his
hand and Theringer just brushed the fingers. The crime reporter was a thin, stooped man with a naked face and scalp.
He had the hot, ancient look of a desert animal, and he
might have been in his early fifties.

"Don't order a martini, Mr. Robbins. Gus makes a lousy
martini. He puts vermouth in it."

"I'll just have a beer," Dave smiled, slipping into the
booth.

"One of the boys, huh?" Theringer grunted. "Personally,
I like bourbon. Bourbon's the only goddam original Ameri-
can art form there is. And who the hell are you to Annie
Gander?"

"Nobody. I mean, I just wanted to find out more about
the case. There hasn't been a word about it in the later
editions."

"Damn right. And there won't be, until those fatheads
in the detective bureau give the go-ahead. They got a lead
on a suspect, and they ain't talking until they dig him out."

"Really?" Dave said politely. "Whom do they suspect?"

"Don't give me that whom crap. I went to school, Robbins, even if I can't write girdle ads." The reporter stuck his
pink head into the aisle. "Hey, Gus! One more and a beer!"

"I think we better start all over," Dave said. "In the first place, I'm not even sure that this Annie Gander is the woman I'm thinking about. Maybe if you could give me a description—"

"Hell, I can paint you a portrait. Black hair dyed blond, baby-blue eyes, a fat fanny, and a bellyful of hooch. What's the matter, kid, didn't your mother tell you there were women like that?"

Dave swallowed his annoyance. "Did you say blond?"

"I didn't say indigo. Listen, what's this all about, pal? What's your interest in this cheap dame?"

"Cheap? The address isn't so cheap."

"Okay, so maybe she comes high. But cheap is cheap, buster, you're talking to Father Time."

Dave looked more closely at the bitter man across the table, and decided that there must have been a woman in Max Theringer's past. Whatever wound she had inflicted was still throbbing.

"I'm serious, Mr. Theringer. I'd like an accurate description. The woman I'm thinking about is young, maybe in her early twenties. She's around five-feet-ten, silver-blond hair, good-looking, but kind of hard, with too much makeup. She might be a showgirl or an ex-showgirl. She had a beaded bag with her initials on it in gold, or gold-colored metal. Now —how close is that description to the murdered woman?"

"On the button," Theringer said sourly, and looked up as the thick-wristed waiter sloshed their drinks on the table.

"Even down to the beaded bag?"

"I dunno anything about the bag."

Dave frowned. "Without the bag, I could have described ten thousand women in New York."

"That's your fault, pal."

"Look," Dave said, leaning forward. "Let me tell you something else. About a week ago, I went visiting a friend out in a suburb called Sword's Point. I got knocked off the railroad platform in front of the train, and just managed to get back in time. Hairbreadth. Perils of Pauline stuff. Five seconds more, and let's not even *think* about it."

"So?"

"I didn't think it was anything but an accident. That's how it looked then."

"But now you think different?"

"For a reason. Last Thursday, I took a pill. It was an innocent little white pill, supposed to be a tranquilizer, and skip the jokes. Only I didn't get tranquilized at all. I got sick as a dog. If I didn't upchuck whatever the hell it was, I wouldn't be bothering you or anybody today. I don't think that was any kind of accident."

"I get it. You think you're on somebody's must-kill list?"

"I can't prove anything. I took the pill bottle to a laboratory and the goddam analysis cost me half a week's pay. But the other pills in the bottle were legitimate."

"And you think all this has some connection with Annie?"

"I've got my reasons. They're hazy, sure. Maybe I'm seeing shadows, or maybe somebody wants my hide for a different reason. There's a guy in the office, for instance, a guy that's feeling mighty bitter about my getting a job he wants."

Theringer was laughing, silently, but with obvious enjoyment. "Murder on Madison Avenue, huh? Make a hell of a nice Sunday feature, pal. Don't forget to give me the scoop."

"You don't believe this, do you?"

"I think maybe it's too much television, friend. Or too many tranquilizers."

"You stink," Dave said quietly. "You really stink, Theringer. If it wasn't for my gentle nature, I'd give *you* the original American art form—a punch in the nose." He stood up.

Theringer's reaction was surprising. "Sit down," he grinned. "I got a photograph."

"What?"

"A picture. Nothing you'd want to frame, but it ought to tell you what you want to know." He reached into his jacket, his face suddenly pleasant. "It's a shot we took of the body, for the files. Nothing we'd ever print."

Dave reached for the glossy in the reporter's hand, and saw what he meant. Annie Gander's body was not the sort of thing you wanted to see at the breakfast table. The bullet wound was in her throat, and the effect wasn't pretty.

But now there wasn't any doubt in Dave's mind— Annie Gander was the woman he had seen at Hagerty Tait.

"Okay," he said. "Now let's talk."

"Sure you want that beer?"

Dave grinned. "Hell, no. I'll take a martini. As long as Gus puts vermouth in it."

When the doorbell sounded in Dave's apartment at nine that night, he only partly expected the visitation he found in the doorway. He knew that it would be Janey, of course. They spent most of their stay-in evenings at Dave's place, since Janey shared hers with two giggling and curious females. But he wasn't prepared to find a Janey decked out in her best whispering satin, instead of the customary sweater-and-skirt.

He blinked at her and said: "Say, what's the occasion?"

She laughed, and even blushed moderately. They sat on the sofa, and Dave scratched his stubbly cheek and felt grimy in his rumpled sports shirt and unpressed slacks.

Then he told her about Annie Gander.

She listened in puzzlement, not sure he was serious, as he outlined his conversation with Max Theringer. But when he mentioned the mysterious hundred and twenty-five thousand again, and Annie Gander's visit to the office, she burst out with:

"Listen! You're not trying to connect Uncle Homer with this murder—"

"No, no," Dave said hastily. "As a matter of fact, the police have their man all lined up, according to Max."

"And who's that?"

"A rough customer by the name of Willie Shenk. One of Annie Gander's many boy friends. Handsome Willie, Max calls him, but I don't know why. He had the tip of his nose cut off in a gang fight, and never bothered to have it repaired. Sounds like a real old-time hoodlum."

"Played by James Cagney."

"No, the genuine article. Spent ten years in prison, and it probably wasn't enough. The police think that Annie and Willie Shenk had a lovers' quarrel."

"And where is he now?"

"He packed up and left. It's obviously more than a coincidence that he left town just when his girl friend gets shot. The police are keeping that out of the story, to keep him off guard."

Janey shivered. "Uncle Homer couldn't get mixed up with people like that."

"I didn't say that. But the whole business has me worried. Especially after that pill business—"

"What pill business?"

He opened his mouth and then closed it again. "Nothing. Hey, look, I've got an idea. Since you're so dressed up, suppose I change clothes and we go out some place? Maybe dancing. Now that Uncle Homer's paying me so much money—"

"All right," Jane said wearily. "If you want to."

"You don't sound very enthusiastic."

"Should I be? I guess it's a good idea—since I *did* dress up. It was stupid of me."

"What was?"

She looked at the floor. "When you phoned me tonight, about coming over—you said you had something important to tell me."

"Well, I did. I mean, I think this business about Annie Gander *is*—"

"Never mind, Dave."

He was just starting to shave when he realized what she meant.

The idea of calling upon Gordon and Grace Tait didn't occur to Dave until late the next afternoon. The account man had been out of Masters Pavilion less than a week, but he was still prisoner to his bed. It was doubtful that he would welcome a visitor, but Dave felt an urgent need for more pieces to the puzzle.

When he called the Tait home in Sword's Point, Grace's maid called her to the phone.

"I know it's an imposition," Dave said humbly, "but what I have to talk about to Gordon is fairly important."

Grace sounded doubtful. "I don't know what to say, Mr. Robbins. Gordon would love the company, of course; he's bored silly. But he must avoid any excitement—"

"I won't excite him. In fact, I may bore him even more."

She laughed. "All right. See you at nine then."

A plans board meeting occupied the rest of Dave's afternoon. He sat at the far end of the conference table, watching the agency president expound his views, thinking private thoughts about Homer Hagerty, and wondering what dank and subterranean depths there were to this gentle-spoken white-haired man who ran the company.

He had dinner near the Terminal, and went to the newsreel theatre until train time. The trip to Sword's Point had a soporific effect.

The estate of Gordon and Grace Tait had once been a segment of the most exclusive area in Westchester County. Now it had fallen victim to an altered zoning law, and the taxi that carried Dave to their door bypassed a number of thickly settled communities. But the cluster of development homes only served to emphasize the magnificence of the Tait home. Half a mile of paving sliced through lush grounds; the house itself rose like the white ghost of a southern mansion. Dave almost expected to be greeted by snowy-haired colored servants, and see Grace Tait herself, hoopskirted and gently languid, on the front porch.

Instead, he found the mistress of the Tait household wearing velvet pants, a tailored shirt, and an armful of African silver bracelets. And there was less than southern cordiality in her greeting.

"You won't stay too long?" she said. "Gordon hasn't looked well all day. He's much weaker than he thinks he is."

"I won't," Dave promised. "Just a few business matters I want to straighten out, Mrs. Tait. Heard anything new from the doctors?"

"Dr. Dishman was here yesterday. It seems that there's really nothing they can do for him now. He's left me some medication; nitroglycerin pills or something, in case Gordon feels worse. Would you like a drink?"

"I don't think so. This is a lovely place you have, Mrs. Tait."

Her face brightened. "Thanks. Maybe you'd like the fifty-cent tour?"

"Not right now. Perhaps after I talk to Gordon—"

"Of course. His bedroom's on this floor; we thought it would be better than upstairs. The stairs, you know."

"Sure," Dave said.

He followed her across a pasture of thick-napped carpeting that trailed endlessly across the large living room. There was a showplace quality to the furnishings of the Tait home; it might have been a model-room exhibit roped off in a department store. There were no ashes in the ashtrays, no dents in the chair seats. The carpet itself was so uniformly smooth that his passage across it left footprints marking his trail.

Grace pulled back a sliding door to a comparatively small room in the east wing of the house, a room that might have served as maid's quarters. There was a different kind of fastidiousness evidenced here: it was a sickroom rather than a bedroom, inspired more by the *Medical Journal* than by

House and Garden. In its center, neatly tucked into the middle of an oversized bed, lay Gordon Tait.

"I'll leave you two alone," Grace said sweetly. "If you need me for anything, just give a shout." She slid the door shut again, her bracelets clinking.

"Ho, Athos," Gordon said.

"Hi." Dave Robbins grinned and pulled up the chair beside the account man's bed. One look told him that Grace's progress report hadn't been exaggerated. If anything, Gordon seemed feebler than he had in the early days of the attack. The skin of his face was tight and colorless, his eye lacked brightness, and his tongue kept moistening his paper-dry lips.

"Sorry to bother you like this," Dave said. "It's not as if we had any real problems—"

"That's okay, Davey-O. Want to hear all about things. That wife of mine is a regular jailer; I don't even get to see the newspapers any more. You couldn't smuggle me in a copy of *Ad Age,* could you?"

"Plenty of time for that. Same old news, anyway."

"Well, what's the poop from the office? You meet old Cubby yet?"

"I met him."

Gordon chuckled. "You don't have to tell me. I can see the scars. What'd he call you? Davy Jones?"

"Crockett."

"I'm Gordon the Warden. Very charming fellow, Kermit. Just an old country boy with an eighty-foot yacht and a taste for long-legged showgirls—"

The reference jarred Dave. "Showgirls?"

"Surprised? Say, the stories I could tell you about Kermit Burke—"

"Wait a minute. Did he know a gal named Annie?"

Dave didn't think it was possible for Gordon Tait's chalky face to become whiter than it was. But somehow, the last trace of color seemed to disappear as Dave asked his question. It was like looking at the bloodless complexion of an animated corpse.

"Gordon, you all right?"

The account man didn't answer, and Dave grew alarmed. He started to his feet to call Grace, but a bony hand slipped out of the bedsheet and dropped restrainingly on his arm.

"No. Sit down."

"I think I better call your wife—"

"No, Dave. I'm all right."

"I didn't come here to upset you, Gordon. It's just that —well, I ran into a little situation."

"Who did you mean? Annie who?"

"The name is Annie Gander. I don't know anything about her, really. All I know is that she's—"

Dave stopped. If just the mention of Annie's name could produce such an effect upon the sick man—what would happen when he spoke of the murder?

He changed his tone. "Well, I'm just curious," he said flatly. "I saw her in the agency the other day, and she seemed upset about something or other. She came to see Mr. Hagerty, and was raising a rumpus with Celia. That's all there was to it."

"You're lying." Gordon's eyes fixed him, and Dave tried to look innocent, without success.

"No, I'm not. I did see her. The only thing is—"

"What?"

"Well, I took it upon myself to go through your Burke files. Even the personal files you kept on the account."

Gordon's eyes were on the ceiling. "What did you find?"

"Well, nothing very important. I figured the files would be good background for me on the account—all those letters between you and Burke, for instance. The only thing that bothered me was this business of a hundred and twenty-five grand paid out to somebody or some organization listed as A.G. I got curious, naturally. I went up to see Sheplow, and he told me that it was strictly an agency expenditure, not charged off to Burke. He also said it was none of my business, but that's Sheplow for you."

"And you think A.G. is Annie Gander?"

"It seemed logical. I was going to ask Mr. Hagerty about it, but then I got to thinking. What if Annie Gander was some kind of—" Dave flushed. "Well, I don't know Mr. Hagerty that well. If this were some kind of personal expenditure, that was his business." He stopped. "Hell, I didn't mean to go into this so deeply, Gordon."

"Go on," Gordon said wryly.

"Well, that was my first idea. I made the mistake of mentioning my ducky little theory to Janey, and almost got my head torn off. And besides, I couldn't figure out why Mr. Hagerty's—personal finances should be included in a Burke folder. You see what I mean?"

"I see. So what was your next theory?"

"I stopped having them, until I saw Annie Gander in the lobby. That started me worrying again. And then there was this pill business—"

"What pill business?"

"I can't swear it was the pills; the lab I took the bottle to couldn't find anything wrong with 'em. But all I know is, I got damn sick in the office one afternoon, sick enough to die. Fortunately, I tossed whatever it was with the rest of my cookies, and I was okay. But I can swear someone was trying to poison me, Gordon."

Tait looked at Dave, and he was either smiling or wincing. His lips were drawn back tight. "Do me a favor," he said with an effort. "On the bureau over there. A little plastic bottle, with capsules. Give me a couple."

"Sure," Dave said quickly.

When he brought the medication and a glass of water to the sick man, Gordon jiggled the capsules in his palm and gave him a tortured grin. "Hope *these* aren't poisoned," he said, and swallowed them.

"Sure I shouldn't call your wife?" Dave said, worried. "I'm not doing you any good with this talk—"

"I'm all right. Just a precaution."

"Look, I don't want to burden you with my problems. Hell, you've got your own. If anybody *did* slip a mickey into my Miltown, it could've been for entirely different reasons—"

"All right," Gordon said.

"What?"

"I think you ought to know the story. I think you've got a right."

"What story, Gordon?"

"It's your problem now, too. Homer should have told you about it; it's not fair to keep you in the dark."

"That suits me. I never did like the dark."

"You know how this whole business started, the baby campaign?"

"Sure, Joe Spiegel told me. Great campaign."

"It's great, all right," Tait said hoarsely. "Only it has its problems. We had two families all set up, you know, only one of them goofed. So we went along with the Clarke baby."

"I know; I saw your letter to Burke."

"Everything was great. The baby was born right on schedule, and we started shooting pictures. The response was nothing short of sensational. I've handled food accounts for fifteen years, Dave, but I never saw a reaction to an ad like that first Burke ad got.

"The second ad, when the baby is born, was even more sensational. We knew the idea had clicked. Old Cubby Burke was in seventh heaven. Factory sales shot up. That doesn't mean the stuff moved out to the consumers, of course. We'll have to wait to find that out."

"The Nielsen people are coming in this week," Dave said. "They're giving us a preview of the market study before Burke sees it. I'll give you a ring and tell you about it."

But Gordon, staring at the ceiling, didn't seem to care about the market study.

"Everything was great," he repeated. "The account was really secure for the first time. We were rolling, for the first time."

He paused and licked his lips.

"Then it happened. Don't ask me how, I can't tell you. The Burke Baby was as normal a brat as you could find."

Dave's hands and feet went cold.

"One day, the kid was a happy, gurgling little monster—

the next day he was a puking wreck. We got a doctor we could trust, but all he did was give us a shrug and a tut-tut."

"But what was it?"

"I don't know. Some kind of meningitis. The kid didn't even last three days after it hit."

Dave's shoulders slumped, and he remembered the strained atmosphere in the home of Irma and Howard Clarke.

"We were frantic. I mean *frantic*. We had only prepared seven ads so far in the campaign, and we had planned to continue it until the Burke Baby was well into his junior foods. If we had to go to Kermit Burke and tell him that both the Burke Baby *and* the campaign were dead—we might as well cut our throat."

"Rough," Dave said. "Those poor Clarkes—"

"Don't give me that crap. Sure, it was rough on the Clarkes. But kids pop off all the time; that's the way the world is. Only to have *this* kid pop off was a major tragedy. Remember, the basic idea of the whole Burke campaign was *health*. Look at the bouncy Burke Baby! Look at the rosy cheeks! Look at the happy smile!"

"But I don't understand, Gordon. We shot the last ad only two weeks ago—"

"Sure you did. So now you know what we had to do, Davey-O. We had to get ourselves a reasonable facsimile, and fast. We had to provide ourselves with another Burke Baby in a hurry."

"Another baby? You mean a switch?"

"Of course I mean a switch! The Clarke kid was four months old when it died. We had to find a baby around the same age, that looked enough like the original to pass. And besides—you know how kids change. Every day they look different when they're that small. We figured nobody would even guess."

"But I don't see how—"

"Use your head, Davey-O. Look at the situation from the Clarkes' point of view. First of all, they're broken-hearted about the loss of their child. So when we talked about getting 'em a new kid to take Donald's place, they jumped at it. Oh, maybe not the woman. Mrs. Clarke kicked up quite a fuss, but Howard was more reasonable. There was money involved, too, of course; a lot of it. Howard Clarke works for the city; he never made more than eighty-five bucks a week in his life. So after we argued the subject a little, the Clarkes took the only sensible course—and took the new Burke Baby into their home. And don't think they don't love the little fella—"

"But where did it come from? The new Burke Baby?"

"We didn't kidnap it, don't worry about that. We just conducted a little investigation, and found a kid born out of wedlock. The mother wasn't too unhappy to part with the little bastard, especially for certain considerations. About twenty-five grand, to be specific."

Dave whistled. "But it's risky. If anybody got hold of the story—"

"That was the chance we had to take. But we figured that the only people who knew about the switch were people who couldn't *afford* to let the story get out. Seven of 'em, all in all."

"What seven?"

"Well, the doctor who attended the baby, first of all. The first Donald. But we made sure we could trust him; we found a few highlights in his medical career that couldn't stand too much attention."

"That's blackmail."

Gordon looked at him pityingly. "You use words too freely, Davey-O. As for the other six, they include Irma and Howard Clarke, Homer Hagerty, myself, and now you. And, of course, the Burke Baby's mother."

"Kermit Burke doesn't know?"

"Not a thing."

"And the kid's mother—"

Gordon Tait collapsed limply against the pile-up of pillows behind his head, chuckling behind closed teeth. "Annie Gander, of course. Good old Annie Gander."

VI. Time to Re-Tire

He overslept the alarm and tried not to look guilty when he arrived at the office at eleven, but his unexplained lateness seemed to have reduced Louise to something close to panic.

"Oh, Mr. Robbins!" she said breathlessly, her mouth quivering. "Mr. Hagerty's been trying to get you all morning—"

"All right, Louise, I'll give him a call."

"Celia said it was *very* important," his secretary said, wringing her hands.

"Don't worry about it, it's not your fault." He took the telephone in hand. Louise was still hovering over him, looking terrified, and he couldn't help saying: "For God's sake, Louise, it's not the end of the world!"

She gasped, put a fist in her mouth, and wheeled out of the office. He knew she would be snuffling in another minute, so he decided against phoning and went to Hagerty's domain in person.

The president was frowning when he walked into the office, but the frown didn't seem to be related to Dave's lack of punctuality. There was something else on the president's mind, and it took five minutes of pointless small talk to bring it to the surface.

"Dave, this is a funny business," he said, looking past him to the window. "It's a business of decisions, and lots of them. Sometimes the decisions are easy, and sometimes they're tough. But the important thing is to make 'em, right or wrong."

Dave said nothing.

"I've made a few lulus in my lifetime. But I've never regretted them, not even my mistakes. Know what I mean?"

"Not exactly."

"Been in this business for thirty years. Lord & Thomas, Ayer, Sterling Getchel . . . I've been around, Dave. And one of the ways I've been able to survive was by my ability to judge people. Nothing more important in the ad racket. But sometimes, you get tempted by your own personal feelings—"

The president locked his fingers on the desk blotter and looked like a physician breaking bad news.

"Dave, I made a mistake," he said candidly. "It was a valid mistake. I liked you and your work so much that I thought you were ready for any job in this business. To tell you the truth, I was being selfish."

"Selfish?"

"That's right. Because I saw myself in you, Dave, myself as I was twenty years ago. Cocky, smart, a real hotshot, ready to tackle anything. I didn't know the true value of maturity and experience. And then there was Janey—"

"What's she got to do with it?"

"Janey's family, Dave. That made you family, too, and it's only natural for a man to look favorably on those he loves—"

Dave scraped back his chair. "This mistake you're talking about. You mean me?"

"Don't put it that way. It doesn't mean you failed, not in the least. It just means that I was so eager to see you succeed, that I handed you a burden too heavy for you. It's not your fault, Dave, believe me. I take all the blame."

"I don't get it. Did I do something wrong? Is the Burke account in trouble?"

"Not yet, Dave, but there are signs, omens. And before we *both* get hurt, I'm taking you off the account."

"What?"

Hagerty appeared to have a stomach ache.

"This hurts me, Dave, really hurts me. I staked everything on you, you know that. But look at the odds. You only had a few years in this business; you're not used to the kind of problems a major account offers. Maybe if Kermit Burke had been a different type of person—"

"You mean Burke wants me off?"

"He hasn't said it, not in so many words. But I know the old bastard, Dave, and I know when he's getting ready to spit flames. I don't want you to get burned when he does."

Dave's right foot had gone to sleep. He stomped it on the carpet, creating an angry emphasis to his words.

"You sure that's what it is, Mr. Hagerty?"

"Uh?"

"You sure that's the reason I'm off the account?"

"Don't misunderstand me, Dave. If it was up to me, I'd stick with you till hell froze over! But don't get the idea I want you out of the shop. You'll still be on the Baked Goods account, and maybe you'll take over on Sugar Babies when Ross—" He paused, and Dave finished the statement.

"When Ross takes over Burke. Is that it?"

"Don't be difficult, Dave. Harlow Ross has been in line for this job when you were still in uniform. I was sticking my neck out for you when I jumped you over his back. Naturally, he'll take over."

Dave stood up. "Is that it?"

"I can see you're taking this the wrong way—"

"Hell, no. It's your agency, Mr. Hagerty."

"You won't do anything foolish?"

"Who, me? I can take orders, Mr. Hagerty. I had six years' experience, remember? I'm still a corporal at heart."

Hagerty chuckled, and came around the desk to clap the young man on the shoulder.

"Not for long, Dave, not for long. Stick with me, and you'll be a four-star general before you know it."

"Yes, sir," Dave said, stiffening to attention.

He stopped at Janey's drawing board before returning to his office. She didn't look up long enough to see the high color in his face.

"You still sore at me?"

"Sore?" the girl said icily. "Why should I be sore?"

"I dunno. But I want to talk to you about something. Free for lunch?"

"I thought I'd eat in."

"Eat out. This is important."

"All right," she said.

"Pick you up at noon."

Harlow Ross was sitting in Dave's swivel chair when he entered his office, sucking an unlit pipe and reading Dave's copy of *Printers' Ink*. The symbolism of the act was crude, and Dave growled his greeting.

"Been looking for you," Ross said smoothly, getting out of the chair. "I figured by now you'd be looking for me."

"I've got nothing to see you about."

"Oh, heck, Dave, I know how you feel." His handsome mouth lifted in a sweet smile. "Look, fella, if you'd like a nose to punch, why not try mine?"

Dave looked busy, riffling through the contents of his IN box.

"I just want you to know that it wasn't my idea," Ross said. "This Burke business, I mean. Hell, I was surprised as anybody when Hagerty told me about it this morning. He would have told you first, of course, if you were in earlier—Do you believe me?"

"Sure."

"You probably don't. You probably think I did you dirty or something. But you're wrong, Dave. Know how I got it figured? I figure Kermit Burke has it in for you. Who knows? He'll probably do the same to me."

The telephone rang, and for a moment Dave thought Ross was going to pick it up. He reached over and snatched at the receiver.

"Mr. Tait calling," Louise said.

Dave covered the mouthpiece. "Do you mind, Harlow?"

Ross grinned, and moved out of the office.

"Hello, Gordon," Dave said.

"Thank God I got hold of you," Gordon Tait still sounded sickly, but with surprising tremulous strength. "I called you earlier but you weren't in. I was hoping—"

"What is it, Gordon?"

"Dave, why didn't you tell me? You must have known about it yesterday, when you were here—"

"Gordon, you don't sound well—"

"You could have told me!" The account executive's voice, once a beautifully controlled instrument, was now shaky and out of pitch. "You knew I hadn't seen the newspapers —I didn't know a thing about it, Dave, not a thing!"

"About what?"

"About Annie Gander!"

Dave grimaced. "I'm sorry; I didn't think it was the right time to talk about it. But that's what really made me curious about this whole thing. Her murder."

"Murder! Oh, God, Dave, I didn't know anything about it! You know that. I'm a sick man. *Sick*."

Dave looked at the receiver in befuddlement. "Of course I know that, Gordon. I didn't say—"

"I warned Homer from the beginning! I told him that it was risky. That woman would have bled us dry, Dave; she was the type. You don't know how tough that kind of woman can be—but I never sanctioned anything like this, Dave. So help me God."

"Gordon, take it easy. You shouldn't be getting upset like this—"

"Just remember what I told you, Dave. When they start asking questions. I just went so far and no further—"

The voice cracked, and Dave said: "Don't talk about it,

Gordon! For God's sake, think of yourself. You're not supposed to get worked up—"

The admonition seemed to do some good. Gordon Tait's next sentence was spoken in a calmer mood.

"The police," he said. "That's the only thing to do now, Dave. We'll have to call them and tell them everything. That's the only sensible course, you can see that. All the rest of this business, about Burke, the campaign, that doesn't matter so much. The important thing is for them to *understand*."

"Maybe you're right," Dave said. "But I think you ought to go easy on it, Gordon. Get some rest, and we'll talk it over later."

"All right," the voice on the phone said flatly.

There was a pause, and a final click.

They found Lucia's restaurant surprisingly quiet, and a waiter found Dave and Janey a secluded booth in the rear. The scene was candle-lit and intimate, and more suitable for romantic conversation than for the speech Dave had prepared to deliver.

"Now listen close," he said, touching Janey's cold hand and pinning it to the table. "Don't say anything until I'm finished. What I have to say won't make me any more popular with you, but it has to be said."

"Go ahead," the girl answered, her eyes hooded in the candlelight.

"You were the one who knew the truth first, Janey. You saw it the day the culls came back from the photographer, when you realized the Burke Baby looked different. And you were right, sweetie, you were dead right. It wasn't the Burke

Baby. It wasn't the Clarke Baby. It was a *real* Little Stranger. Name of Gander."

Her fingers quivered under his grip.

He kept on talking, holding fast to her hand as if its release might break the continuity of what he had to say. He told her about his visit to Gordon Tait, and what the account executive had revealed. He told her carefully and factually, trying not to editorialize. Then he said:

"It's obvious what happened, Janey. They paid Annie Gander twenty-five thousand for her part in this business. *Not* a hundred and twenty-five. That was another payment. And you know why that was made."

"I don't."

"Blackmail. It couldn't have been anything else. Once Annie Gander realized her power, she got smart. Maybe her boy friend Willie put her up to it. But she really put on the pressure, 'bleeding them dry,' Gordon called it. She was in a position to cost them more than just the Burke account—she could cost Hagerty Tait its entire business life. The scandal would end the agency for good."

"You said them."

"What?"

"*Them.* You're including Uncle Homer in all this, aren't you?"

"Honey, I'm not a prosecuting attorney. Of course your uncle knew about this; Gordon spelled it all out for me. The decision was made mutually. But the important thing is what happened afterwards: a blackmailing woman, with a hoodlum boy friend, who was out to see that they didn't make a dime of profit for all their hard work . . ."

He stopped talking as a rotund waiter beamed over them

and requested their wine order. When Dave said "whisky" he frowned and shrugged his shoulders in great sadness.

"All right, maybe it's true," Janey said. "But it's not really a crime, is it? For heaven's sake, Dave, there've been worse hoaxes in advertising. What kind of business do you think this is?"

"Look, let's not get academic—"

"Academic?" A flame flashed in her eyes. "Listen, do you know who our real heroes are? That smart guy stuck with all the white salmon when everybody wanted pink salmon. The guy who advertised 'Guaranteed not to turn pink in the can.' That's your advertising hero for you. Or those rotten medical specialists—you could fill Johns Hopkins with them! The ones who gave America B.O. and halitosis and dishpan hands. And then there's the subliminal jokers—"

"Cut it out! You know it's not that simple, Janey. For every wise guy there's a hundred honest joes in the business. We don't all keep salmon from turning pink—"

"This holy attitude of yours! God, that's what really gets me! Just for a lousy advertising trick—"

"I'm not talking about that!" Dave said angrily. "I'm not talking about advertising. I'm talking about murder!"

"One *whisky*," the waiter said contemptuously, planting the glass in front of Dave and stalking off.

"What are you saying?" Janey asked quietly.

"I'm talking about murder, honey. That's what I'm worried about; the murder of Annie Gander. I got a telephone call from Gordon—"

"You told me the police had their man. You said it was a Willie somebody, a hoodlum—"

"I said the police were looking for him. There's no real

proof that he did the killing. But let me finish. I got a call from Gordon. He was practically hysterical; I've never heard him like that before. It seems he just found out about Annie Gander's death; I hadn't told him about it on my visit to Sword's Point. And he was terribly afraid that he would be involved—"

"What does that prove?"

"I didn't say it *proves* anything. But it made me worried, Janey. If Gordon Tait thinks Annie was murdered for a reason—"

"Well, say it out loud! You're hinting long enough. You think she was killed because of the blackmail—"

"You'll have to admit, blackmail and murder are old friends; they're always hanging around each other."

"But you don't think Gordon Tait did it?" She was speaking too calmly. "Of course not. After all, he was practically on his deathbed when this—this woman was killed."

"Of course not. I know he didn't."

"So that leaves Uncle Homer, doesn't it?"

"Janey—"

"Process of elimination, Dave. Not Willie Shenk. Not Gordon. So that leaves Uncle Homer—"

She started to get up, and Dave's face went angry.

"Wait a minute. Maybe that's not the only murder I mean. Maybe there's another one coming up. My own."

Her eyes went through a quick series of reactions, starting with astonishment and ending with contempt.

"Welcome to the Grand Guignol," she said, laughing unsuccessfully.

"All right! So maybe you won't believe that. But here's something you can check on. Your dear Uncle Homer just handed me the pink slip this morning. He's taking me off the Burke account."

"What?"

"Said I wasn't ready for the big time, like your old boy friend Harlow Ross. But I know better, Janey. He's on to the fact that I know more about this baby business than I should; he's chopping me off before I *really* gum things up—"

"So *that's* it! That's why you're so hot and bothered! You were told to turn in your ulcer, and now you're striking back! I should have known!"

"*Whisky* not good?" the rotund waiter said, as Janey gathered her wraps and stalked off.

"Whisky fine," Dave said gloomily, and picked up the menu.

He had two more drinks, and then ordered lunch. By the time he was through, it was past three o'clock, but he didn't care.

He met Harlow Ross at the coat-check counter, and there was something different about the account executive. Dave couldn't detect it at first, but when Ross greeted him, he realized that there was no sign of the customary pipe.

"Hello, Harlow," he said. "I thought you'd be smoking corncobs by now . . ."

Ross merely frowned and looked preoccupied. Then he said: "Who knows? Maybe I'll cut it out altogether. Maybe it's not too good for me."

"That doesn't sound like you, Harlow."

"Well, after what happened to Gordon—makes you think. We don't take enough care of ourselves . . ."

"Gordon's okay. I just spoke to him this morning."

Ross looked pained.

"Well, don't look so surprised," Dave said. "Medical science is wonderful. Don't you read *Reader's Digest?*"

"You spoke to Gordon today?"

Dave blinked. "Sure, around eleven. Why?"

"Then I guess you didn't hear—"

"Hear what?"

"Gordon's dead," Harlow Ross said nervously, and pulled a pipe from his overcoat pocket.

VII. *Never Underestimate the Power of a Woman*

Deference.

That was the word, but it didn't occur to Dave until several hours after he walked into the offices of Hagerty Tait the next morning. Yet from the moment he stepped into the Early American lobby, it should have been apparent that something had changed in the attitude of the agency employees. Jody, the receptionist, heightened the candle power of her smile the instant he stepped from the elevator at ten-thirty. Wilson, the agency's TV man, stopped him in the hallway to ask his opinion of a new package show. Wilton Sheplow, the agency treasurer, cracked the concrete façade of his face in a friendly smile when they met in the men's room. Louise, his secretary, seemed more awed by Dave than ever.

The only member of the Hagerty Tait organization that

seemed unchanged was Janey Hagerty. The door to her office remained shut to him.

He was puzzled by the altered atmosphere, but not for long. The first clue was the flat package lying on his desk blotter.

He picked it up and weighed it in his hand. It was heavy. With a paper knife, he cut the string that bound it, and pulled the brown paper aside.

It was a silver-framed photograph of Kermit Burke. The baby-food manufacturer was grinning with all the freckled charm of a latter-day Will Rogers, and there was a corncob in his right hand. Scrawled across the bottom of the picture were the words:

"To Davy Crockett, affectionately, from Cubby."

He studied the picture, without understanding its import, until he looked up and saw Homer Hagerty in the doorway.

"Well! I see you got the Medal of Honor."

"I don't get this," Dave said. "What's *he* sending me a picture for?"

"Figure it out for yourself." The president smiled, a little sheepishly, and took the deskside chair.

"I can't. Unless old Cubby believes in farewell presents for his ex-account men."

"Never mind the *ex*," Hagerty said. "Things have changed around here since yesterday, Dave. That picture ought to give you the tip-off."

Dave put the photo on his desk, shaking his head. "Beats me. I thought I was canned off the Burke account."

"I had things wrong. I had it figured that Burke didn't like you, Dave. But when I paid him a visit yesterday afternoon, and told him my plans, the son of a bitch almost threw me out the window. He insists that you stay on the account. Of course, I was delighted, especially now that poor Gordon—" He sighed, as if to indicate that his joy was not totally unmixed with sorrow.

"Off again, on again," Dave murmured. "It's a little unnerving, Mr. Hagerty."

"Well, that's the crazy business we're in. But I don't have to tell you how pleased I am, Dave. I never was so happy to be wrong about something in my life."

Dave looked at him sharply. The smile was uncertain on the president's face, the lines around his mouth taut. Was Homer Hagerty really so glad?

"So that's how things are, Dave. And just to make sure there are no hard feelings, I'm getting Sheplow to sweeten the pot a little. Figure on another two grand per annum. It won't make much difference, with taxes and all, but maybe it'll buy some canapés."

He got up slowly and went to the door. Then he turned and said:

"Speaking of our pinup boy, Dave—we've got a date to see him tomorrow morning. Wants a rundown on the Nielsen sales analysis. Okay?"

"Sure," Dave Robbins said.

He sat at his desk for the next half-hour, trying to reorient himself to the new state of affairs. He was too jolted by the switch even to feel a proper sense of sadness or loss in the death of Gordon Tait. As a matter of truth, he was feeling elated.

Louise buzzed him. "Countess on the line."

Dave punched the plastic button that brought in the call.

"David? Guess who is in my office."

"Can't imagine, Countess."

"Silly man, won't you even guess? It's Sonya. I persuaded her to come into town for the day, and what do you think happened? A dear friend of ours gave us two tickets to *The Circled Heart*. You know how impossible it is to get seats."

"So I've heard. Hope you enjoy it, Countess."

"No, no, I can't even *think* of going; I have a directors' meeting tonight. I'd appreciate it if *you* would escort the dear girl."

"Well, I'm sort of in a bind myself. We're meeting with Mr. Burke tomorrow and—"

"Now don't tell me you have to work all night! I simply won't believe it, David. Besides, Sonya would be simply heartbroken if you refused." Her voice became girlish. "You know, I have a suspicion that Sonya is rather *sweet* on you."

"It's impossible, Countess. Some other time, perhaps."

There was a pause, and Dave knew she was simmering. But he no longer cared; he looked at Burke's photo and felt power.

When she spoke again, her voice was deadly calm.

"Were you planning to come here this afternoon? About the Cincinnati contracts?"

"I thought the end of the week—"

"I won't be available the end of the week. I think you should come this afternoon."

"All right," Dave said curtly. "I'll be there at two."

He glowered in the back seat of the taxi all the way to Long Island City. When he entered the baking plant, Jorgenson greeted him amiably on the iron staircase that led to the executive floor, but he answered only with a grunt.

He paused at the door of the Countess' office, steeling himself for his client's disgruntled manner, and for his reunion with Sonya.

He was wrong about both. Sonya wasn't in the office, and the Countess' manner was painfully pleasant.

"Sit down, David. I missed you last week."

"Things have gotten pretty hectic, Countess. I suppose you heard about Gordon Tait."

"Ah, yes. My own poor husband was carried off by the same ailment." Then she smiled. "But let us talk of more pleasant things. Sonya was thrilled when I told her about tonight. I thought it would be sweet if you took her to dinner. I took the liberty of making reservations for you at Voisin's; they'll expect you at seven. And please, David, don't be annoyed by your foolish old Countess, but I've taken care of the bill in advance—"

"You what?" Dave blinked. "Listen, Countess, I don't think you understood me—"

"I knew you didn't mean what you said."

"But I did!" His lips tightened. "I don't think you had any right to tell Sonya that. Now you'll just have to tell her the truth."

"I wouldn't dream of it. You may not know this, David, but Sonya is a very *delicate* girl. Not that she's *unhealthy*, mind you. Strong as a bull!"

"I'm happy for her. But tonight's out of the question."

"It would upset her terribly, David. She thinks a great deal of you."

"You told me. But I didn't tell you something, Countess. I'm—sort of engaged to somebody."

"To Miss Hagerty?"

She smiled, and Dave started.

"I think you are perhaps deluding yourself about that one, David." She seemed to be amused. "From what I hear, she's not as interested as you might believe."

"From what you *hear?*"

"I hear a great deal, darling. I have great big ears and great big eyes, like the wolf in the nursery story." Her smile widened, showing great big teeth.

"I'm glad you're so well informed," Dave said, the blood making his cheeks burn. "But the truth is, I'm not interested in your daughter, Countess. She's a lovely girl, but that's the truth. You can do what you please about it."

She lost some vivacity for a moment, and then brightened. "I see. Your new position on the Burke account, it's given you fortitude. Isn't that so?"

Dave's flush deepened.

"I hesitate to do this, David. But I believe you need a lesson in humility."

He watched her slide open the top drawer of her desk, and remove two stiff sheets of paper.

"Charming, are they not?"

He took them from her. They were photographic culls, one sheet containing pictures of the Burke Baby taken by Ray Smalley, the other containing photos of the Burke Baby taken by Bob Bernstein.

"What's the point, Countess?"

"If you look closely, David—"

"Come to the point!"

"Only a fool would fail to see the difference in those infants, David. I am not such a fool."

"Where'd you get these? The last time I saw them they were in the art department—"

"The question is unimportant. The point is that I have them. The retouched photographs were cleverly done, but these are most self-explanatory. Surely you must know the effect they would have upon Mr. Burke, and the results of his realizing that there has been a deception . . ."

"They have a dirty word for what you're doing, Countess."

"Then don't use it. All I ask of you is a little affection, a little attention for a poor girl that has no friends and no—" She stopped, and snatched the culls from Dave's hands before he could damage them. "That wouldn't help, David; of course I have others."

"You're pretty good at this business."

"Necessity, they say, is the mother of invention. And I, too, am a mother."

"I've heard of shotgun weddings before, but this—"

"I never said marriage, David. Only attention. Later, we can see—"

"Goodbye, Countess." He picked up his attaché case. "You can do what you like with the photos. I had nothing to do with the switch in babies, and I can always get another job if we lose the Burke account. But I won't have my love life arranged for me, not even in royal fashion."

"David!"

He opened the door and left.

In Manhattan, he stopped at a bar called Puccini's before going back to the office, and then called Louise and asked for any messages. There was one. A Max Theringer had called, and wanted him to return the favor.

He called the *Times-Express.*

"Theringer," the nasal voice said.

"Max? This is Dave Robbins."

"Oh, yeah. Thought you might be interested in this. Our friend Willie Shenk's in town, and wants to talk to me. A strictly hands-off proposition; he just wants to tell me his side of the story."

"Shenk? Annie Gander's boy friend?"

"That's him, Handsome Willie. A third party is setting up the meeting. I didn't say anything about not bringing friends, so if you want to sit in, maybe you'll learn something."

Dave swallowed hard. His contact with the underworld was limited to balcony seats at gangster movies.

"That's swell, Max . . . Where'll it be?"

"That's one of our problems; we need some place really off-beat. How would your office be, around midnight?"

"Okay, I guess. Nobody works that late."

"Good. See you then."

Dave had dinner at Lucia's, and returned to the office a few minutes past eleven. He worked desultorily, one ear cocked for the sound of the elevator.

They showed up at ten minutes past twelve.

"Hi, pal," Theringer grinned, taking a seat. "Nice hole you got here. Shake hands with Mr. Shenk."

Dave looked at a pale, narrow face, shaped like a white trowel. Willie Shenk's eyes were heavy-lidded, and the lashes thick and black. His mouth was small, but the lips full. He might have gotten the sobriquet of "Pretty Boy" in the crime news, but his nose took care of that. It was oddly truncated, giving him a strange, incomplete look. He didn't seem very dangerous.

"How are you," he said flatly.

"Just fine," Dave answered, dropping into the swivel chair.

"This is just an informal chat," Theringer said. "Mr. Shenk's already filled me on the details. Mind saying it again, Willie?"

Shenk scowled. "Ain't much to tell. I didn't knock off Annie. I ain't the killer type. But I'd like to get my hands on the guy who did."

"What would you do?" Theringer asked mildly.

"Kill him!"

Dave pulled his collar away from his moist neck. Despite Willie's girlish features and slight build, he now appeared to be a genuine menace.

"Tell me about it," he said tentatively. "What happened between you and Annie?"

He scanned Dave sharply. "Just what's your interest, pal? Max here says you didn't know her, but maybe he's a liar. She knew a lot of peculiar types."

Dave squirmed. "No, I didn't know her. I'm just as interested in finding her murderer as you are. For reasons of my own. But from what Max tells me—" He took a deep breath. "The cops think you're the one. You saw Annie last. You had opportunity. You probably had motive."

"Nuts. I been shackin' up with Annie on and off for the past eight years. Only in my line of work, I can't have no regular home life, you know what I mean? Annie was always talking marriage, but I didn't go for it. That don't mean I didn't like her—"

Theringer interrupted. "You wouldn't exactly call her faithful, though, would you, Willie? She had her share of boy friends."

"I knew that," Shenk said, with dignity. "I didn't begrudge her nothing. All I asked was that she keep her nose clean when I was in town. That ain't much to ask, is it?"

"No," Dave said affably, "that isn't much."

"And did she?" Theringer asked.

"What?"

"Keep her nose clean this time? Or did she maybe cheat on you a little bit. And did you fight about it?"

"No!"

"Then what about the baby?" Dave said bluntly.

"What baby?"

Dave blinked. "You mean you didn't know about Annie's child?"

"Max told me about it. Only like I said—I been outa town a lot."

"So you wouldn't know the father?"

"It could be half a dozen guys."

"Like who?"

"Don't ask me," Willie Shenk said.

Dave said: "Did she ever say anything about an advertising agency named Hagerty Tait? A man named Homer Hagerty, or Gordon Tait?"

"Never heard of 'em."

Dave sighed. "This isn't helping much."

Max Theringer leaned forward. "Look, Willie, this was your idea. I'll help you if I can, but you got to stick to the facts. The police got it all figured that you killed Annie, and with your record, you're a cinch for a conviction. So let's open up a little."

"Don't bug me, pal." Willie Shenk narrowed his eyes at the reporter. "I'm telling you all I know. I left the apartment two days before Annie was bumped. We had a little argument—"

"About what?"

"About dough. I didn't like the looks of her setup. Annie was too loaded; I figured she still had a rich boy friend on the string. Once in a while, I'd spot some guy comin' out of the building; she always said she didn't know him. We had some words one night, and I belted her. Not hard, not where it would show. But she got pretty independent since a couple of years ago. She told me to beat it. So I beat it."

"And that was all?"

"That was it. I didn't kill her, Mr. Theringer. That's the truth. I'll tell you something funny; I really liked that dame. I liked her a lot."

The pale, narrow face, with its odd, foreshortened nose, took on a strangely pathetic expression.

"Okay," Max Theringer said. "I'll see what I can do for you, Willie."

Willie stood up. He wasn't very tall, nor very wide. But there was a bulge under his left armpit which made it clear that muscles weren't everything. He looked around the account executive's office with interest. He picked up a layout of the new Burke ad, and shrugged at the greeked-in headline. Then he lifted the picture from Dave's desk, and his mouth fell open, showing badly repaired teeth.

"Him," he said.

"What?" Max looked at Dave.

"This is him, for Chrissake. The guy who was hanging around the place. This is the guy!"

Dave took the photo from his hand, and took a long, refreshed look at Kermit "Cubby" Burke.

VIII. *You Press the Button, We Do the Rest*

He took a Seconal at two A.M. and resisted the sleeping pill until four. When the strident sound of the alarm urged him out of bed at eight, he went groaning into the bathroom and took a Dexedrine out of the cabinet. He watched himself swallow the pep pill, and said aloud:

"Okay, pills. Fight it out between you."

In the back of the taxi inching its way across town, the Seconal seemed to be victorious. Dave slumped against the cushion, his head nodding, and the driver had to "Hey, bud" him awake at the entrance to the office building. With groggy generosity, Dave handed him a tip almost equal to the fare.

He didn't reply to the elevator starter's meteorological inquiry, or to the receptionist's good morning, or to his secretary's sad-eyed greeting. The first word he uttered, hoarsely, was:

"Coffee!"

Louise responded like an army corpsman advised to bring the blood plasma. She telephoned the coffee shop downstairs and stressed the emergency nature of the order. In five minutes, a white-coated young man came down the hall with the brisk authority of a surgeon. Saucer-eyed, Dave yanked the cardboard cover from the cup and took the first life-giving sip. Louise watched him in trembling anticipation.

"Aaah," Dave said, in gratitude and relief.

The day had started.

"Mr. Hagerty call me yet?" Dave asked. "We were supposed to see Burke this morning."

"Oh, I forgot. Celia called and said the meeting's been postponed until Monday; Mr. Hagerty was called out of town. But he asked if you would make sure the proof of the new ad is ready to be presented. And something about the Nielsen sales report; she said you would know what he meant."

Dave grunted. If he had known of the postponement, he would have spent the morning in bed.

"All right," he said. "Ask Miss Hagerty if the proof's ready. No, wait a minute. I'll go ask her myself."

He picked up the coffee container and bore it down the hallway towards Janey's office. The door was still closed, and he knew why, but he turned the knob and went inside.

Harlow Ross was at Janey's drawing board, intent over the layout pad, with a grease pencil in his hand. He looked up with a swiftly fading grin, and then flipped the pad shut.

"Hi, Dave," he said sheepishly. "Just leaving a little note for Janey."

"She's not in?"

"Not yet. Say, I meant to talk to you about this Burke business. I know you'll think I'm kidding, but I was real happy to hear that old Cubby wants you on his team. Understand he sent you a picture of Our Founder?"

"That's right," Dave said curtly. He didn't feel like facing Ross' determined joviality that morning. "Leave a note for me, too, huh? Ask Janey to call me."

"About what?" Janey said, coming up behind him. She was carrying a tweed topcoat over her arm and swinging a leather bag from her other hand.

"Well, this is something," Dave said. "Since when do I beat *you* into the office?"

She brushed past him, and Harlow, smiling like the Queen's favorite courtier, rose from the chair and took the coat from her hand. He hung it up behind the office door, and then held the chair for her in front of the drawing table.

"Guess you two have business," Ross said amiably. "So I'll toddle along. If he gets fresh, Janey, just yell."

Janey reacted woodenly to his attentions, and when Ross closed the office door after him, she set about whittling a pencil with the grimness of a Maori warrior preparing a spearhead. Dave watched her for a moment, and said:

"Don't worry, this is legitimate business. Uncle Homer wants me to make sure the Burke proof is all ready for Kermit. We're presenting it tomorrow."

"It's in the studio, being mounted."

"Oh." He took a sip from the coffee container, not wanting to leave. "Care for some of this?"

"No, thank you."

Dave grimaced. "Listen, don't you think you're carrying this sorehead act a little far?"

"The ad's in the studio," Janey said. "Was there anything else you wanted?"

"Yes, damn it!" He slammed the cup to the top of her taboret, making a brown tidal wave that splashed over the formica. "For one thing, you can turn over the Burke Baby photographs to me. I'm still on the account, you know, even if Uncle Homer doesn't like the idea. And I want to take charge of the photos, all of them, right from the beginning of the campaign."

"What for? They belong in the art files."

"I don't care where they belong. I want them for my own reasons. If you'd like to make a federal case out of it, I'll send you an official memorandum."

She blew pencil shavings off her razor blade.

"Well?" Dave said. "What about it? Do I get the pictures, or did Uncle Homer give you orders not to release them to anybody?"

"I don't have the photos," Janey said.

"What?"

"I don't have them. I haven't had them since last week. Somebody took the entire batch out of the files."

"Somebody? Like who?"

"I don't know. I sent a memo around to all departments, asking if anyone had seen them, but I didn't get any reply. Didn't you see the memo?"

"No," Dave said guiltily. There were many memos he didn't read.

"You can check the office correspondence file and read it," she said coldly. "In case you don't believe me."

"I didn't say that."

"You don't say a lot of things. But you *think* awfully loud, don't you?"

"Oh, nuts," Dave said. "This whole attitude of yours is illogical. You're all worked up because of Uncle Homer, because I don't like this baby mess he got me into. I've heard of in-law trouble before, but by God, this is ridiculous. We're not even married yet."

There was the slightest of twitches in Janey's frosty composure. Dave saw it, and then twitched himself.

"What I mean is," he said lamely, only distantly aware of what he was saying, "that we ought to postpone these in-law fights. Until after."

"Until after what?"

"Until we're married," somebody said, using Dave's voice. He listened to it in surprise, wondering how he had lost control.

Janey sat rigidly in the chair, staring at the gray cover of the layout pad.

"Is this what you call a proposal?"

"Who, me? Sure," Dave said belligerently. "That's what I call it. What did you think it was?"

"I don't know."

"Well, it's a proposal, goddam it. I'm asking you to marry me. Now what are you going to do about it?"

She turned to face him.

"Just let me ask you this. Would you like to be married *before* you have my uncle arrested for murder, or afterwards? I think maybe it would be better before. Then we can plan our honeymoon around the time he's executed. It would make a lovely honeymoon trip, up to Ossining. Don't you think?"

Dave opened his mouth, but didn't know what to do with his tongue. He made a gargling sound in his throat, and Janey turned back to her drawing board.

"All right," he said finally. "Then I'll tell you what I'll do for you. I'm going to clear up this whole business, starting Monday. I'm going to make a presentation to Kermit Burke that he'll never forget—"

She glanced up sharply.

"You heard me," Dave said shakily. "We're supposed to have a meeting with our country cousin, to show him the new Burke ad, and talk over the sales figures. But I'm going to show him more than that. I'm going to show him that he's been in the middle of a three-ring circus. I'm going to tell him about the Clarkes, and Annie Gander, and Gordon, and the whole switch routine. Then we'll see what happens."

"Why should he believe you?" Janey whispered.

"I'll *make* him believe me. The photographs aren't the only evidence, don't worry about that. There are people who can corroborate the story. Maybe not you, or Uncle Homer, but there are people."

"Like who?"

"Like Countess Szylensca," Dave said, the color mounting in his face. "She didn't have any trouble getting photos. You didn't know about that, did you?"

"I don't know what you're talking about. What's the Countess got to do with this?"

"Plenty, more than you know. And there's one other thing you didn't count on. Even if Uncle Homer thinks he covered the trail, he's wrong. Don't forget about Bob Bernstein, the guy who took the pictures. The negatives are still on file in his studio, so I can get myself a nice new set, just for the asking."

"Bernstein's dead."

"But Mrs. Bernstein's not. So if anybody wants to know where I am today—"

Janey was flipping the pages of her layout pad angrily, the milk-glass composure of her face totally shattered. Dave, who had been attempting to create that effect since he walked in, now felt guilty. He let the color fade out of his cheeks and walked over, hand ready for a tender gesture.

"Oh, hell, Janey, let's leave the molehills alone. We don't have to let this thing make a difference to us."

"Hasn't it already?"

"Look, we can talk this all over, nice and cool-like. Maybe tonight—"

She was reading the scrawling uphill slant of Harlow Ross' handwriting on her pad.

"Not tonight," she said. "I'll be busy tonight."

Dave peered over her shoulder. The words read: *Guess who has tickets to The Circled Heart this evening? Your ever faithful, Harlow. How about it?*

Dave stiffened. "All right," he said, in a bruised voice. "If that's how you want it."

He was breathing hard on his way back to his office, and feeling as if the Dexedrine tablet was finally emerging champion. He slammed into his swivel chair with such force that a caster fell out of one leg. He replaced it, and then sat in the chair, drumming on the desk blotter as if it were a kettledrum in a burlesque house. Finally he picked up the telephone and asked the operator to dial Countess Szylensca's office.

"Yes, David?" Her tone could have iced the wire between Long Island City and Manhattan.

"I've been thinking it over, Countess, about what we talked about yesterday. I think maybe I was a little hasty, and if Sonya isn't *too* sore at me—"

"Sore? Why, David, Sonya could never be displeased with you!"

"Well, that's just fine. You tell Sonya that I'd very much like to see her tonight, and if she can manage to get into town—"

"She won't have to manage anything. She's been staying in my apartment since yesterday. You can pick her up there."

"Good, I'll do that. You tell her I'll be around at seven. Okay?"

"Wonderful," the Countess said, plainly thrilled. "And about the tickets. If I call my friends at the theatre before noon, perhaps I can—"

"Never mind about the tickets. And you can skip the dinner reservations, too. I'll handle my own date, if it's all right with you."

"Of *course* it's all right, David. I never meant to—"

"Sure, I know, Countess. Then I'll see you both around seven."

He hung up, in mixed satisfaction and gloom. Then he called Louise in.

"I'll be out for the rest of the day," he said. "Do me a favor and get the Burke proof from the art department when it's mounted. Have the mailroom wrap it up for Monday's meeting, and tell them to drop this into the package." He took the blue-bound Nielsen sales report from his top drawer and handed it to her.

"Will I be able to reach you?" Louise said.

"No. Only in case of emergencies, and I mean *emergencies*, like the building falling down. I'll be at Sword's Point, visiting Mrs. Bob Bernstein."

On the 12:28 that lumbered out of Grand Central, Dave looked down the row of empty seats and realized that he had practically become a commuter without the privileges of suburban residence. It hadn't been many days ago that he had made a similar journey to Bob Bernstein's modest ranch-type, and the interim had been punctuated by three deaths—including Bernstein's own. A heavy depression, its storm center located in his stomach, settled over him at the thought.

But there were other ingredients in Dave's gloom cloud. His bold idea of exposing the Burke Baby hoax in Monday's meeting now seemed rash and unpromising. There were too many elements he didn't understand; most of all, Willie Shenk's surprising revelation about seeing Kermit Burke in Annie's vicinity. What had brought them together? The whole point of Annie's blackmail was to keep them apart, to prevent Kermit Burke from ever discovering her relationship to the cooing infant in the baby food ads. It didn't make sense.

Yet Dave knew he would go through with it. He felt a compulsion to bring the truth into the open and see the reaction it would create. As long as there were secrets, he would be chained to too many doubts and fears. *The truth,* he thought wryly, *shall set you free.*

And then there was Bernstein's widow. Ruth Bernstein, a cozy little woman with the features of a middle-aged Madonna, had sounded pleased and cheerful on the phone, but he dreaded the prospect of facing her. He hadn't called once since her husband's death, hadn't even performed the ritual of sending a sympathy note. What would she think when she realized that his visit was selfishly motivated?

He felt even worse when he got off the train at Sword's Point, and saw her short-legged figure in the parking lot, standing beside a gray Morris Minor. She waved to him, and smiled when he was close enough to appreciate the greeting

"I told you not to bother meeting me," he said, mildly chastising. "I could have taken a taxi."

"I didn't have anything else to do. Hope you don't mind this baby buggy."

She got behind the wheel and he sat beside her, knowing that he should say something about Bob, something brief and consoling. She was wearing a green cardigan over a flower-printed housedress, and a jeweled comb in her straight black hair. She didn't appear to be in mourning, so he rationalized himself out of saying anything. It was only when they reached the Bernstein ranch house, a modernistic brick-and-redstone structure that was actually no more than a glorified bungalow, that he saw where her grief had been deposited. The house itself was in mourning. The shades were drawn in every window, and the shutters were closed in the bedroom area. The lawn was unweeded, overgrown, ragged. When they entered, even the light she flicked on in the outside hallway didn't evaporate the gloom.

They sat in the dim living room, facing a curtained picture window. "Would you like a drink?" Ruth asked. "I'm having one, in case you want to know."

"All right," Dave said.

She brought two glasses and a bottle and placed an ice bucket between them on the free-form coffee table. Then she sat on a plastic chair that had a hole in it, and kicked off her low-heeled shoes with a sigh.

"I can see what's going on in your mind, Dave," the woman said, her eyes wise. "You think you have to make a little speech or something, about Bob. Listen, you can forget it. I've heard all the little speeches already, and they don't help much."

"I'm sorry."

"So all right, that's all you have to say. You're sorry, and I'm sorry. Finished."

"I know it's not a good time to bother you, Ruth, and I really wouldn't if it wasn't important."

"Please. I'm glad for the company. People are afraid of me now, like I'm going to cry at them or something. Believe me, I won't cry."

"It was such a shock. I know how terrible it must have been, happening so suddenly—"

"You probably don't even know *what* happened, do you?"

Dave felt guilt. "No, not really. There was just that item in the paper, about the accident."

"If I could only have been there," Ruth said dreamily. "If I hadn't gone away—"

"You weren't home when it happened?"

"No. Not that I could have helped; I don't know about such things, all that fancy equipment he kept in his studio and darkroom. You know where he worked, in that reconverted barn behind the house?"

"Bob showed it to me."

"Nothing to see now. It's all gone, everything. I never thought photography was a dangerous profession, like a truck driver or something. You take a camera, you push a little button, what could be so dangerous?" She sipped her drink.

"Where were you, Ruth? When it happened?"

"I was in the Bronx, at our old neighborhood. My mother still lives there, in the same apartment building. She never really approved of Sword's Point; it was a little too *goyisher* a place for her. So just that day I had to decide to pay her a visit. I didn't think Bob would need me for anything. I knew he was going to be busy, with his portrait appointment . . ."

"Portraits? Did Bob do portraits?"

"Listen, that's how he started in this business. In his father's portrait studio, in the Bronx. It was only later that he got into this fancy advertising stuff. But when he lost the Burke Baby Food job, he wasn't so reluctant to accept portrait assignments again. So when he told me he had a portrait sitting for that afternoon, I figured fine, perfect, just the time for me to see Mama."

Dave put down his glass. "Let me get this straight, Ruth. He took this picture on the day of his—on the day the accident happened?"

"Yes, that's right. Somebody called and made the appointment that morning; Bob took the call himself."

"Do you know who it was?"

"I have no idea."

"Man or woman?"

Ruth shrugged.

"What time was it? The appointment?"

"I don't know. But the accident—they figure it must have happened around four-thirty. They asked the neighbors, the police I mean. One of them said they heard a kind of muffled explosion around then. So that's how they figure it. I got back home around seven, and the barn was already a cinder. Bob was in the darkroom. He wasn't even human any more, so burned and broken—" Her voice choked off for a moment. Then she added quickly: "No crying, I promised you."

"But what happened? What caused it?"

"I'm not sure. They said it might have been what they call spontaneous combustion. The crazy chemicals he kept around got overheated and blew up. They said he didn't suffer, that he was dead right away, but I ask myself, how do they know? How do they know anything?"

Dave looked at her. She wasn't keeping her promise.

"The whole place smelled bad, the way I used to think hell smelled. Everything was in a mess, broken, torn to pieces, burned. It was like a bomb dropped on us. I got to thinking lately, maybe we made a mistake, taking a house so far away from people. The nearest house is a mile away; maybe if we were closer they would have heard the noise and come over. Maybe if he wasn't dead yet—" She shrugged her shoulders. "In the Bronx it couldn't happen, I'll tell you that. The whole borough would have been at our door in two seconds. In this place, a house blows up and people go on cutting the grass."

Dave waited for her to continue. When she didn't, he

said: "How much was destroyed, Ruth? Everything? Pictures and everything?"

"What can I say? There was nothing worth keeping, believe me. I had the whole mess cleared out."

"Then it's all gone? The negatives he used on the Burke account, and all the other things?"

"Why? Was it important?"

"No," Dave said wearily. "Not that important. To tell you the truth, I was hoping they'd still be intact; there's something I wanted to do with them. But skip it, Ruth, I can manage."

"I'm sorry, I didn't realize. Was that what you wanted to see me about?"

"No, no," Dave said painfully. "Not just that, honest. I wanted to see you, find out more about what happened. It's just that I've been running into a lot of problems lately—"

"You mean on the job?"

"Yes, sort of." He refilled his glass. "Ruth, could I ask you just one more question?"

"Certainly."

"This portrait business. The two things coming together like that— Didn't you or Bob keep any record, outside the studio maybe? Couldn't you find out who came here that day?"

"Records?" She blinked at him. "Not really. Bob didn't get so many jobs he needed records. Why?"

"No reason. I just wanted to know."

She bit her lip. "I never thought to wonder about it too much. The person never called back; they probably heard about the accident later. For all I know, the film's still in the camera."

"What camera?"

"It was one of the few things I kept, after it happened. I don't know why; I was so angry at the studio I wanted to break everything that wasn't smashed already. But I kept the camera, Leica—"

Dave slid to the edge of his chair.

"Could I see it, Ruth? If you don't mind?"

"Sure, of course."

She got up and disappeared into another room. He waited tensely. When she returned with the Leica in her hand, he took it and turned it about in puzzlement.

"How do you tell if it's loaded?"

"There's a little gizmo here—" She indicated the place. "See the marker? Yes, it's loaded; there's film in it."

"Ruth, would you mind if I took the film?"

"No. But why, Dave?"

"Just out of curiosity. Could I?"

"Sure. Here, I'll unload it for you."

She turned out the one lamp in the room and snapped open the case. She unrolled the film out of the camera, sealed the gummed end, and handed it to him.

He didn't want to stay any longer, but he didn't know how to leave. But Ruth Bernstein must have sensed his restlessness, because she offered him the means.

"Are you busy, Dave? At the office?"

"Yes. Very busy. As a matter of fact, I better get back there before closing time; there's a man I have to see."

"I understand. It was good of you to come, Dave."

The return trip was excruciatingly slow, despite the fact that the train ran on schedule. At Grand Central, he telephoned the office and spoke to the manager of the agency's art studio. The manager gave him the name of a photography firm on Forty-fourth Street where emergency development was available. He walked rapidly across the Terminal to the Forty-second Street exit.

He got prompt attention at the studio, by the simple expedient of using the agency name. They asked him if he would care to wait in the lobby, and he said yes. He picked up a copy of *Photography Annual* and tried to concentrate on the pictures, but his own focus was inadequate. He was thinking too hard about what Ruth Bernstein had told him, and about the alarming idea which had burst in his brain like a flash bulb the moment she mentioned the portrait appointment.

By the time the darkroom timer bell rang, Dave's thoughts had taken him in only one direction. If his reasoning was correct, the film in the developing pan would show the portrait of Bob Bernstein's murderer.

The door opened.

"Tough luck," the aproned young man said. "Somebody must have opened the camera before the roll was finished. It's all overexposed, Mr. Robbins."

He handed over a soggy pack of sheets, as blank and uninformative as jokers in a pack of cards.

IX. The Skin You Love to Touch

The glamorous pueblo that was Manhattan Manor loomed over the East River Drive, creating a landmark for tugboat captains and a fine sightseeing spectacle for the residents of Welfare Island. The apartment building was even more impressive at night, and Dave watched the approach of its floodlighted terraces through the taxi window with the special awe that a citydweller feels for his city. The building affected everyone. The cab driver touched his cap at Dave's moderate tip, and the doorman opened the De Soto door with Cadillac grandeur. The glass portals of the entrance were swung open with a majesty worthy of visiting royalty, and the deep-piled carpet in the lobby greeted Dave's feet softly and with humility. The elevator operator ushered him solemnly into the padded cage, and deposited him gently on the floor of Countess Szylensca's residence. The splendor was almost hypnotic, and if somebody hadn't been cooking cabbage in an adjoining apartment, Dave would have remained prisoner to its spell. As it was, he wrinkled his nose and grinned, then pushed the button that rang chimes inside Apartment 18-A.

A dusky young woman carrying an overnight suitcase answered. She giggled when she saw him, and then traded places with him. He looked baffled when she closed the door after her, and then Countess Szylensca's voice, at the far end of the hallway, explained.

"That was our maid, Dessie. She was just leaving when you rang. Come in, David, dear."

He went down the foyer to the main room, and saw red. It wasn't a retinal trick; the room was red-carpeted, red-draped, and red plush in general. The furniture was pale ivory, and would have cost plenty even in the century it had been made, but everything else was red. "Gee, you know what," he said. "I've got a great name for this room, Countess. Why don't you call it the Red Room?"

The woman laughed uncertainly, and beckoned him closer with her cigarette holder (black). The Countess Szylensca had decided to be statuesque that night. She wore an antique gown of money-green. Her hair was piled precariously high on her head, adding a height she didn't need. She handed him a cocktail (red) when he was close enough.

"Manhattan all right?" she said. "Sonya likes Manhattans, too, I discover. If you want the truth, I think all she really cares for is the cherry at the bottom." She laughed and sat down. "I'm afraid Sonya isn't accustomed to our wicked world yet, David. Sometimes I think she was born in the wrong era."

"Er, where is Sonya?"

"Getting dressed; she'll be ready in a moment. She's in a tizzy of indecision, of course, about what to wear. And how have *you* been, David?"

"Oh, fine, Countess, considering everything."

"You're still angry with me, aren't you?"

"Angry? Why should I be?"

"About yesterday, of course. Those photographs. I know you'll never really forgive me for what I did, David, but I don't think you'll regret your decision."

"Now wait a minute." Dave lowered his drink. "Let's get one thing straight, Countess. My being here tonight has nothing whatsoever to do with your little stunt yesterday. If you want to carry your little photo album to Kermit, you've got my permission. As a matter of fact, I'll take it to him myself, if you want to hand it over."

The sizable eyes of the Countess enlarged.

"I'm here because I want to be here," he said. "Not because I was blackmailed into it. So let's get that settled right off the bat."

"But that's wonderful, David! You don't know how happy I am to hear you say that—"

"Good for you," Dave said. "Now would you please tell Sonya to get her zipper zipped. I haven't eaten since breakfast, and frankly, I'm starved."

The Countess looked positively thrilled at Dave's masterful tone, but she didn't rise.

"Where were you planning to go tonight? There are so many wonderful places in the city that Sonya hasn't—"

"Never mind about the wonderful places." Dave stretched out his legs, and then, on second thought, propped them up on the bowlegged marble table in front of him.

"There's a joint on Third Avenue I like, and that's where we're going. They don't have any red plush, but the wine's red and the spaghetti's good. And it's also reasonable. After that—well, maybe I'll take Sonya to the movies."

"Of course," the Countess said, almost panting in admiration. "Sonya loves the movies."

"Well, maybe we *won't* go to the movies. Maybe I'll take her bowling."

"I don't think Sonya even knows what bowling *is*, but I'm sure she—"

"Well, I don't know exactly *what* we'll do after dinner. All I care about now is getting my face fed. So if you don't mind, Countess, I wish you'd tell your daughter to snap it up."

She got up and swished to the arched doorway, returning a minute later with Sonya in tow. It was apparent that the girl had been ready some time before, and that the instruction to delay had come from her experienced mother. The wax museums had never produced a glossier figure than Sonya Szylensca looked that moment. Every soft black curl had been glued into place. The satiny blue dress, ballooning at sleeve and skirt, was molded to her thin frame to emphasize her fleshless ribs and, Dave realized, surprisingly voluptuous bosom. The Countess had obviously applied her superb color sense to Sonya's thin face, and the result was startling. Her skin was phosphorescently white, her mouth fire-engine red, her bright lavender eyes brush-outlined in black. She was a beauty, all right, and Dave was properly appreciative. But she was still unreal, unearthly, a watercolor instead of a woman.

"Hi," he said brusquely. "Ready to go?"

She nodded shyly.

"Have a wonderful time, dear," the Countess said, pecking the air around her daughter's cheek. "I'll be going out myself around nine, and I may not return tonight at all." She looked at Dave. "Some silly meeting's been called; I may have to spend the night at a hotel. But I don't really mind."

"Good night, Countess," Dave said, taking Sonya's arm and steering her towards the door.

"Take care of my little girl," the Countess said gaily. "And have fun, children."

Sonya's lashes remained at half-mast throughout the down trip in the elevator. She didn't raise them until the taxi completed the circuit around the fountain in the courtyard, and took them into the more mundane atmosphere of York Avenue. Then she turned an innocent gaze in his direction and said:

"Where are we going, Mr. Robbins?"

"Call me Dave, Sonya, nobody calls me Mr. Robbins. Except my mother, of course."

"What's that?" She blinked rapidly, and then must have realized he was attempting the light banter she read about in novels. She laughed briefly, and cleared her throat for a small-talk effort of her own.

"It's too bad you couldn't make the play last night. It was very good."

"Really? What was it about?"

The blush was evident even in the darkness of the back seat.

"Oh, love, I guess."

"Imagine that," Dave said.

When they entered Lucia's restaurant, Dave turned in his hat and coat at the checkroom, and didn't complain when the headwaiter selected a table more conspicuous than most. Sonya wasn't hard to be seen with, and if there was the smallest chance that a certain blond art director and her pipe-smoking escort wandered in . . .

Sonya was looking at him. "What a charming place," she said. "Do you come here often?"

"On occasion. I recommend the veal scaloppine, and the spaghetti, of course. They make it very thin and brown here, with a fine light sauce. You don't count calories, do you?"

"Not really," Sonya said. "But I don't know if I can eat very much."

She promptly proceeded to disprove herself. Dave watched two old-fashioneds, half a dozen bluepoints, a dish of spaghetti, a large order of veal scaloppine, a quarter-loaf of bread, two glasses of Chianti, a dish of tortoni, and two demitasse coffees disappear, daintily but relentlessly. He was a trifle abashed at her display of appetite, but when it came time to pay the bill, she sat back as demurely as ever, with eyes lowered, looking pale and unfed.

"What would you like to do now?" he said. "We can either go to the movies, or take a hansom around the park, or sit around some smoky joint until morning. Which would you like best?"

"I don't know," she said timidly. "What would *you* like to do?"

"Frankly," Dave said, frowning, "I'd like to go some place where I could take my shoes off and loosen my belt. But this is your night, Sonya, so you name it."

She didn't answer for a moment. Then she said: "Why don't we go back home? We can listen to music or something. Or maybe you'd like to play Scrabble again?"

Dave didn't let her hear his groan.

"Sure, fine," he said. "Let's do that."

They were back at Manhattan Manor not even three hours since their departure, but it was only when Sonya turned the key in the lock that Dave remembered how conveniently the apartment had been deserted. The maid had been discharged for the evening, and the Countess was attending a fortuitous meeting that would detain her until dawn. It almost seemed arranged.

But any suspicions about Sonya's intentions were quickly erased by her actions. She set about efficiently turning on every available light, and then made good her promise about the Scrabble game. She opened the board atop the coffee table in the Red Room and then squatted on the crimson carpet, busily turning over the little white tiles in the box. Dave said: "Want me to mix us a drink?"

"Not for me," she said cheerfully. "My head's still buzzing. But you help yourself."

Dave helped himself. He brought an ice-laden glass of Scotch to the sofa and sat down with a sigh, uninspired by the prospects of the word game.

"Think it's too warm for a fire?" he asked.

"Oh, I think a fire would be lovely. Do you know how to make one?"

"I'm not sure. Something about rubbing boy scouts together." He got up and went to the fireplace. There were three pressed logs and some crumpled paper in readiness.

He applied the flame from his cigarette lighter, and the blaze started.

"That was easy," he said. Too easy, he thought.

She was still busy with the tiles, amusing herself by spelling out words on the colored squares of the playing board.

"Sonya," Dave said.

"Yes?"

"Mind if I ask you a question?"

"Certainly not." She looked up, her eyes excessively bright. For a moment, Dave thought they reflected the flames of the fire, but then he saw they were generated by an inner warmth. They made him vaguely uncomfortable, but he went on.

"Did you ever notice any baby pictures around the apartment?"

"What kind of pictures?"

"Baby pictures. Whole sheets of them, the kind we call culls. Usually about a dozen to the page."

She pursed her mouth.

"No, I don't think I have. Why?"

"No reason." He returned to the sofa. "Okay, so let's play Scrabble. I'm still smarting over that defeat you handed me at Romanvilla. You play a mean game, Sonya."

"All right." She got to her feet. "But I don't think we need all these lights, do you? The fire makes the room so bright."

She had kicked off her shoes, and did a barefoot dance around the Red Room, flicking off the lights she had so carefully turned on a few minutes before. When she came back, she was laughing and panting with her exertion, the surprising bosom heaving. "My, it's warm!" she said, slipping off the abbreviated blue-satin bolero. Sonya had shoulders that were remarkably creamy.

"Shall we play?" Dave said gruffly.

She sat on the sofa, giggled, and gave him a sidelong coquettish glance that was new to him.

"Sure you want to?"

"Of course. I'm after revenge."

"Some things are sweeter than revenge," Sonya said.

"Like what, for instance?"

She giggled again, and flung herself against the back of the sofa.

"Why not see for yourself?"

He didn't know what she meant until her eyes dropped in the direction of the Scrabble board. At first, he didn't make any sense out of the words she had spelled out. When he did, he gasped as if struck by a faceful of ice water, and read them again. They read the same way on his second look, and he was shocked all over again.

"Hey," he said feebly.

"What's the matter?" Sonya tittered.

He had seen the words before, but never in such circumstances. They were short, pungent words of ancient origin, and wouldn't have given Sonya many points in a Scrabble game.

"Why, Sonya," he said, with a meek laugh that came out of his throat like a cackle. "I never thought you were that kind of a girl."

"Oh, but I am," Sonya said, her voice gone husky. "That's exactly the kind of girl I am, Dave." She extended an arm towards him.

"I don't get it." He let himself be drawn to the seat beside her. "You seemed so . . . different."

She put her hand on the back of his neck and slipped two fingers into his shirt collar.

"I thought you wanted to get comfortable," she said.

"I did, but—"

"Then why don't we *both* get comfortable, Dave?"

Something went *crack!* in the fireplace, and Dave leaped to his feet.

"Better watch those logs; don't want to set the house on fire . . ."

When he turned back to her, she was lying full-length across the sofa cushions. He headed for the wing chair opposite, but she crooked her finger at him.

"Come on over," she said.

"I thought you wanted to play Scrabble," Dave said petulantly.

She arched her back. "Come on over, Dave."

"Look, Sonya, you're really a very nice girl, but I think maybe you had a little too much to drink—"

"Don't be silly, that was hours ago. If you're worried about Mama, forget it. She won't be back all night."

"I'm not worried about Mama. I'm worried about you. Now be a good girl and sit up. We'll play one game and then I'm going home."

He came near her and she snared his shirt-cuff. "All right," she said. "We'll play one little game and then you can go home. What's a four-letter word for—"

Dave yanked his arm away. "Never mind. I just thought of a seven-letter word. Goodbye."

"Dave!"

He began a march to the hallway, feeling ridiculous. His hat and coat were on a harp-backed chair beneath a gold-framed mirror. He snatched them up and put his hand on the doorknob.

"Dave, wait a minute." She was in the doorway.

"What is it?"

"I just remembered something." Sonya leaned against the door frame with one hip extended. "I remember those pictures you were talking about. The baby pictures."

He returned to her. "What about them?"

"Put your hat and coat down and I'll tell you."

She watched him obey the command, with her hands behind her back. She backed into the Red Room, tilting her chin and shutting her eyes. He grunted, seized her roughly, and kissed her. Her body didn't feel anywhere near as fragile as it looked.

"Now that," Sonya sighed, "is how I like to play Scrabble . . ."

"What about the pictures?"

"Can't we talk later?"

"We can talk now."

"All right," she said, rubbing her cheek against his shoulder. "Some man came up to the apartment last week and gave them to Mama. They were in a brown envelope with the name of Mama's agency on the outside; I saw it lying on her dressing table. What's so important about them?"

"Who was the man?"

"I don't know. He was sort of cute, like a college professor. Only younger. And he was smoking a pipe; I remember that, because Mama said the whole house smelled of tobacco when he left."

"Harlow!" Dave said.

"What did you say?" Sonya looked indignant.

"Nothing. Listen, Sonya, I just remembered something terribly important. The building is falling down."

"What building?"

"Skip it. I've really got to leave now, believe me. It's been a wonderful evening, and I want to thank you very much."

"But I don't *want* you to leave." She emphasized her wish with a body motion. "I want you to stay, Dave . . ."

"I really can't, honey, honest. For one thing, I promised my mother that I wouldn't touch a woman until I was forty years old."

She pulled away from him and stomped her foot noiselessly on the red carpet.

"You bastard!" she said.

"Why, Sonya! You're full of surprising words, aren't you?"

"You louse! You stinker! You *fag!*"

"That's it," Dave said sadly. "Now you've got my secret. I've just got to get home or Montgomery will be furious. You know how jealous he is."

"Get out of here!" Sonya shrieked. "Get out and stay out!"

"Give my love to Mama," Dave said.

By the time he reached the exit of Manhattan Manor, Dave was filled with an irresistible desire to be alone—preferably in a phone booth. He found one hidden in the rear of a drug store on First Avenue, and went digging into his pocket for a coin. He had only a quarter, but dropped it into the round slot and dialed Janey's apartment.

The telephone rang eight times before he admitted that

she might not be home. He looked at his watch: it was five minutes to eleven. If she had accepted Harlow Ross' offer, that meant she would be leaving the Broadhurst Theatre in approximately fifteen minutes. It wouldn't be easy to spot them in the milling crowd, but it was worth a try.

He scrambled out of the booth, leaving the quarter for the next prying finger, and hailed a cruising cab.

The street outside of the theatre was relatively empty, but it had an expectant look. He was just stepping out of the cab when an usher came racing to the inner door, in a mild panic of preparation for the exiting crowd. Then the people started coming, babbling their critiques of *The Circled Heart*, making the usual competitive bids for taxis. His first sight of the mob was discouraging; all the faces blended into one universal physiognomy. He stood on the edge of the sidewalk, jerking his neck around like a Javanese dancer. A mounted policeman brushed by him, and three women rattled coin boxes in his face. The task seemed hopeless.

Then, for the first time in his life, he was grateful for Harlow's ubiquitous pipe. There it was, a gnarled lump of black oak, stuck like a club between his smiling teeth. Holding onto his arm, looking lovely and much too content, was Janey. At first, he wanted to shout at them, but then decided on subtler methods. He trailed them quickly through the crowd.

The cab situation was desperate. The fleets hadn't been released from the East Side garages yet, and there was a polite pitched battle in the middle of Forty-fourth Street. But Ross didn't seem perturbed, and Dave soon realized why. On the corner of Eighth Avenue, a gleaming black Cadillac awaited his approach, and a uniformed chauffeur was going through his door-opening, good-evening-sir, good-evening-madam routine. He heard Ross say "Serafino's" to the driver, and then watched him climb into the rear of the rented auto beside Janey. Without waiting to see the limousine pull away from the curb, Dave headed south on Eighth Avenue, looking for a taxi. He outran a stout woman and nailed one. "Serafino's," he told the hackie.

Serafino's was a coffee house on Fifty-sixth Street, of a type that specialized in odd varieties of coffee and clientele. Dave had never cared for its uptown-bohemian atmosphere, but he could have guessed that Harlow Ross would like it. When he entered, a pony-tailed hostess jangling with Village jewelry tried to show him a table, but he scanned the customers until he spotted the one he wanted. "I'm joining friends," he said, pushing by her.

Janey saw him first, and managed to disguise her reaction. But Ross took the pipe out of his mouth in order to open his mouth and register surprise.

"Hello, buddy," he said. "What the hell are you doing here?"

"I'm crazy about coffee," Dave said, looking at Janey. "And besides, there's something I wanted to ask you about."

"I suppose you've been following us," Janey said accusingly. "You didn't know Dave was an amateur detective, did you, Harlow?"

Dave pulled up a chair. "That's right. And I'm not doing so badly, either. For instance, I found out something pretty interesting about you tonight, Harlow."

"About me?" Ross blinked.

"That's right. I never knew you had hobbies before. Came as quite a shock."

"What are you talking about?"

"About your little avocation. Pimping for Fun and Profit."

Janey snorted. "He's drunk."

"Or maybe I can use a nicer word," Dave said. "Like spying."

Ross made a loud sucking noise on the pipe stem.

"I just had a little chat with a friend of a friend of yours," Dave said. "She told me about your little visits with Countess Szylensca. About those photographs you delivered to her apartment. How's it work, Harlow? You on a fee basis, or do you get paid per assignment?"

Ross scraped back his chair and stood up. In another era, he might have slapped at his hip and drawn a six-shooter. But being a child of his times, he merely glared at Dave and snapped: "Let's get out of here, Janey. Your friend's getting obnoxious."

She was looking back and forth at them, bewildered.

"What's going on here?"

Dave didn't like being towered over. He got to his feet and took advantage of his greater height.

"Tell her about it, Harlow. Tell Janey how you swiped the photos from her office—"

"You bastard," Ross whispered. Then he made a mistake, underestimating the heat in Dave's furnace. He put out his hand and flattened the palm against the lapel of Dave's suit. It was only a slight, aggressive push, but it was enough to trigger the button of Dave's temper. His right arm performed like a piston, delivering a right cross that was as good as anything on the Wednesday Night Fights. It cracked against Ross' outthrust chin and sent the pipe flying out of his mouth to fall, rattling, among the espresso cups on the next table.

Janey's gasp wasn't heard amid the general brouhaha that followed. The Serafino waitresses descended upon them first, like a company of excited ballerinas. A white-coated man with hairy forearms came from behind the espresso urn to shout Italian invectives at them. The entire coffee house re-acted vocally and enthusiastically to this break in routine, except the two combatants. After the blow was struck, they regarded each other calmly, and then Ross rubbed his chin and spoke to Janey.

"Let's go," he said hoarsely. "Let's get out of this place."

She rose swiftly and took her coat from the back of the chair. They went to the checkroom together, and Ross got his own plaid topcoat from the wide-eyed girl. But before they went out the door, Janey suddenly turned and came back to the table.

"Dave," she said quietly.

Her eyes were placid, and Dave, encouraged, said: "Look, Janey, I'm sorry about this, but what I said was true. Harlow knows about the baby business, and he's been reporting to the Countess—"

"All right." She lowered her eyes, and then her voice. "But what I wanted to ask you was, did you mean what you said this morning? In the office?"

"What I said?"

"About wanting to marry me."

He gulped. "Of course!"

"Isn't it the usual thing, for a girl to get an engagement ring?"

"Gosh, Janey, you mean—"

"I wish you *had* given me a ring, Dave." She looked up quickly, and her eyes flashed more fire than a diamond's. "So I could give it back to you!"

Then she whirled and joined Harlow Ross at the door. They left without looking back.

Dave sat down slowly, and the pony-tailed waitress approached timidly, gathering the money from the table top.

"Did you—did you want something?"

"Yes," Dave said. "Do you make Coffee Cyanide here?"

X. Even Your Best Friend Won't Tell You

"The big, flat package," Homer Hagerty chuckled, as Dave shifted the big, flat package under his arm. "Trademark of the ad man. I don't know how we'd recognize each other without it."

"There's always the gray flannel suit," Dave said.

"No, not any more; anybody with sixty-five dollars wears those. You can't tell a butcher from an account executive these days. Nine, please," he said to the elevator operator.

They were in the outer lobby of the Burke Baby Products Company in another ten seconds. It took less time to make the vertical trip than it did to traverse the twenty yards of green broadloom that stretched towards the double doors of the executive offices. Dave kept his stride matched to that of his employer's, and tried to keep his mind unclouded by the pale cast of thought that would unsettle his resolution.

The receptionist clicked on a fluorescent smile at their entrance. "Good morning," she said brightly. "Nice to see you again, Mr. Hagerty, Mr. Robbins."

"Good morning," Hagerty said. "Want to tell Mr. Burke we're here? He's expecting us."

She spoke into the Hush-a-Phone, and then smiled them towards the red-leather chairs that were pushed against the wall. Dave dropped his burden to the floor and sat down.

"Sure we got everything?" the president said. "Proofs, layouts, that Nielsen report?"

"Everything," Dave answered meaningfully.

Another five minutes vanished into eternity before Kermit Burke's spectacular secretary appeared.

"Mr. Burke is terribly sorry," she said throatily, emoting with her body, "but something came up and he'll be delayed a while. Would you mind waiting just a little minute?"

"A little minute would be fine," Hagerty said. When she left, he chuckled: "That girl makes quite an entrance."

"Her exit's not too bad either."

"Tell you the truth, I'm glad we've got a minute alone, Dave. There's a sort of personal question I wanted to ask you."

"Sure, Mr. Hagerty."

"It's about Janey." He clucked at Dave's facial reaction. "Now I don't mean to meddle in your business, Dave, but you know how close I am to Janey. Anything that makes her unhappy—well, that upsets me, too. And I have a notion all's not well between you."

"That's what I'd call an understatement. But if you're worried about Janey, put your mind at ease. She's got a new playmate these days."

"You mean Harlow?"

"That's right. Iron-jaw Ross."

"What's that?"

"Nothing. Say, this is something new for Cubby, isn't it? Didn't you once tell me he never breaks a promise or an appointment?"

"He's usually pretty prompt, all right. Must be something important if he keeps us waiting. But don't get me off the subject, Dave. Janey spent the night at our house yesterday, and when I saw her at breakfast this morning, I could have sworn she'd been crying. Now I know my Janey, and she hasn't cried since she was eight years old—"

The click of high heels brought their eyes to the doorway. A woman was coming out, but it wasn't Kermit Burke's secretary. It was the Countess Szylensca, and an observer would have been intrigued by the reaction her presence produced on the faces of the two men in the red-leather chairs. They looked like Greek masks: the older man's mouth curving upwards in a smile, the younger man's descending in a frown.

"Good morning, Countess!" Homer Hagerty boomed, in his best pulpit voice. "So nice to see you again."

"Good morning," Dave said glumly. He was thinking rapidly. There could be only one reason for this early morning visit; the Countess must have been talking to Sonya, and whatever version of last night's episode had been reported, it was sure to be unfavorable to Dave. She must have called upon Burke with the express purpose of fulfilling her promise to reveal the truth about the Burke Baby.

The Countess became immobilized when she saw them. "Good morning," she said. "I'm sorry to have delayed you, but there was something important I had to speak to Mr. Burke about. But I wonder—" She looked at Dave speculatively. "Could I delay you a moment longer, David?"

"Sure, Countess."

"I'd like to speak to you. Alone."

Hagerty grinned. "Don't worry about me. I'll go see a man about a dog." He rose and headed for the doorway.

"Well, Countess?"

"David, I think you know why I came here this morning—"

"I suppose so. You just saved me the trouble, Countess, because I had the same thing in mind."

She didn't seem to hear him. "Frankly, I was so upset when Sonya spoke to me early this morning, that my anger was uncontrollable. I wanted to hurt you, David, in the worst possible way. It seemed inconceivable that anyone could take advantage of a girl so pathetically unequipped for the vulgar side of life . . ."

"What's that?"

"Oh, I know what you're thinking. It was a typical mother's indignation, of course; I suppose I've forgotten what it's like to be young and passionate. But somehow, I expected you would be more understanding, more considerate. I'm not really blaming you."

"Now wait a second! Just what do you think happened last night?"

"Please, David, let's not talk about it. Sonya is willing to forgive you, and so am I. I knew how foolish I had been the moment I walked into Mr. Burke's office. I didn't say a word about the photographs; I concocted some other excuse for my visit. So you needn't worry about your little secret; it's perfectly safe."

"You didn't answer my question. What did Sonya say happened last night?"

The Countess stood up. "Not another word about it. We'll pretend it never happened, David." She smiled at him quickly, and squeezed his hand. "Men!" she said, with amused tolerance. "You're all brutes, aren't you? But please, David, *please* wait until you're married, won't you?"

Then she turned and left.

Dave sat transfixed until Homer Hagerty returned.

"Okay, boy, Kermit's ready for us now. Dave!"

"Huh?"

"Stop daydreaming, fella! Curtain's going up."

"Oh, yeah," Dave said. "Sure." He retrieved his big, flat package, and followed Homer Hagerty into Kermit Burke's office.

"Let's hear the good news, boys," Kermit Burke said, excavating tobacco out of the jar with his corncob. He chuckled and looked up slyly. "Betcha don't know how I figured it was good news, did you? Tell you a little secret. When you fellas come in here all smiley, I figure you got something to worry about, and don't want me to know. When you walk in with long jaws—well, that's a sure sign you're bustin' with good news. Right?"

Hagerty blinked in admiration at Burke's dubious psychology, and said: "Guess we can't fool you for a minute, Cubby. Yep, it's good news, all right." He slapped Dave's shoulder. "Davy Crockett here's got the story in his little black bag. Suppose we get right down to it?"

"How about the ad?" Dave said. "Would you like to see the first proof, Mr. Burke?"

Solemnly, Burke lifted the porcelain kitty out of his bottom drawer, and placed it, jangling, on the desk blotter. Dave frowned, and dug into his pocket.

"Haven't got any quarters," he said.

"That's all right, this establishment gives credit." Burke tittered, and leaned back in the chair, locking his hands behind his head. He watched Dave undo the string on the package, and then took the mounted proof of the Burke Baby ad from his hand. He studied it carefully, without comment, and then placed it on the desk. "Let's hear the sales story," he said.

Dave took the blue folder out of the wrapping paper and turned to the first page.

"Of course, this is only a brief summary of the report; the Nielsen people will be giving us the complete story by the end of the week. But here's the basic situation. The total market is up seven percent in all territories. But Burke's share of the market's gone from eighteen percent to twenty-seven percent, representing a nine-percent increase out of a larger total. That's in unit sales; the dollar increase is even higher."

"Let's see that little book," Kermit Burke said.

Dave handed it across the desk.

"Mighty impressive," Burke said, looking up at them from under shaggy, wheat-brown eyebrows. "I suppose you advertising fellas take all the credit, huh?"

"Of course not!" Hagerty said generously. "We feel your own sales department had as much to do with the increase as anything *we've* done, Cubby. Smart bunch of merchandisers, every one of them."

"Crap. You don't really think so, do you, Home Run?" He laughed without opening his mouth. "Truth is, our sales department's been running scared ever since 1954, and you know it. Nothing's changed in our business except the ad campaign; if you fellas want to take a bow, go right ahead. Personally, I give you full credit. What's *your* opinion, Davey?"

Dave cleared his throat.

"I agree with you. It's the advertising, all right. The campaign has done more for Burke Baby Foods than anything else. The trouble is—" Dave paused, and let the earth make one more motion in the cosmos "—the campaign's a complete and utter phony."

Hagerty, who had worn a white-toothed smile since Dave first undid the agency package, didn't close his mouth a fraction. Burke continued to regard him with quizzical, smiling eyes. Dave realized that his announcement came too suddenly for full import, so he said:

"That's right. The Burke Baby's a phony, and so's the whole campaign. There's not a word of truth in it, and I think the best thing you can do now is drop the whole idea. That's my advice, Mr. Burke."

The client's face altered slowly. Then he whispered: "Fifty cents. You owe me fifty cents."

The realization had finally come to Homer Hagerty. His mouth closed, and the skin around his lips became so wrinkled and old that he appeared to have forgotten his teeth. He put his hands on the sides of the chair in an effort to hoist himself to standing position, but he seemed unable to rise. A subtle shade of pink began to spread from the periphery of his collar towards his cheeks. When he opened his mouth again, it was to gargle on the words he was trying to say.

Burke said mildly: "Well, Davey, that's a kind of strong statement. You maybe want to explain yourself?"

"I'll be glad to."

"*Robbins!*" Hagerty bellowed.

"Now you take it easy, Home Run. The boy wants to say his piece, and you let him do it. You know I never shut up anybody when they got an opinion. My gramps always said—" He paused, unable to think of anything his gramps always said. "Go on, Davy Crockett," he grunted. "Let's hear you out."

Dave, having taken the first step off the diving board, plunged right in.

"Take a look," he said, lifting the mounted proof from Burke's desk. "Take a close look, Mr. Burke. The agency art department did a good job of retouching the photos, but you've seen enough pictures of the original Burke Baby by now. See if you can spot the difference."

"What kind of difference?"

"The most important one of all, Mr. Burke. You're looking at a different baby in this ad, because the original Donald Clarke is dead. He died of spinal meningitis at the age of three months, and the agency was too damn scared of losing your business to tell you the truth. Look again, Mr. Burke."

Burke looked, and said: "Don't see much difference, Davey. You think other people will?"

"I don't care what other people will do, Mr. Burke. The

point is, you've been duped. Because the agency didn't make sufficient preparations to guard against this kind of emergency, they did the next best thing. They substituted the illegitimate child of a woman named Annie Gander . . ." He searched Kermit Burke's face; there wasn't a flicker at the mention of Annie's name. "The Clarkes took Annie Gander's baby, and are pretending it's their own. The agency switched photographers, and did everything they could to conceal the deception. But you know what they say about the tangled web, Mr. Burke. You just can't bottle up a secret like this—already too many people know about it."

"Like who?"

"Mr. Hagerty and Mr. Tait knew. The doctor who attended little Donald knew. The Clarkes knew. Bob Bernstein, the photographer, could have known. And now there are others in on it: Countess Szylensca, for instance, and Harlow Ross, and Mr. Hagerty's niece . . ."

Hagerty grabbed his necktie as if it were a python. "Janey?" he said. "Janey knows?"

"Quite a list," Burke said smoothly. "How come none of these people told me this little piece of news before, Davey?"

"Figure it out for yourself. For one thing, three of them are dead. Annie Gander, Gordon Tait, Bob Bernstein. The doctor was gagged by a little sharp undercover work on Gordon's part; he had once killed a girl in an illegal abortion. The Clarkes were silent because they wanted to keep their substitute Donald; I won't even mention the money they stood to gain. As for the Countess, Harlow Ross, and— Janey—well, they've all got their viewpoints. But I forgot one name on my little list, Mr. Burke. Me. I know, and I'm telling you. What's more, I'm advising you to drop the campaign before somebody else gets hurt—"

"Nobody was hurt!" Hagerty said vehemently. "The switch hurt nobody! It was just a business necessity—"

"Take it easy, Home Run, the boy's not through yet. Are you, Davey?"

"Almost through, Mr. Burke. I just wanted to say this. It wasn't easy for me to tell you what I did; I guess it'll cost me my job, and maybe my girl. But it was harder to keep the secret; it was getting foul and smelly, like an old piece of cheese you keep lying around too long. I can't prove anything, but it's my opinion that the secret produced a couple of murders—" He didn't look in Hagerty's direction, despite the outcry of protest the president made. "And I know for sure that it's produced blackmail of several interesting varieties. So I decided the best thing to do was clear the air, Mr. Burke. Now you can do what you like."

He returned to his chair, and waited.

Burke paddled the desk blotter with floppy fingers, looking at him. He picked up the proof of the current Burke Baby ad and examined it once more. Then he picked up a memo pad from his desk and began to scratch at it with a pencil.

"The way I calculate it," he said slowly, "you called me Mr. Burke about eight times, Davey boy. That's another two bucks you owe kitty."

Dave's mouth made an O.

"Is that all you have to say about it?"

Burke grinned slyly, and looked at Hagerty. "Quite a hot-shot you got there, Home Run. What did you ever do to deserve him?"

Hagerty groaned. "Honestly, Cubby, I—"

"Never mind, never mind; we shouldn't have underestimated him, that's all. Shoulda known that a real clever fella like Davey would nose out the facts. Credit where credit's due, my gramps always said."

Dave scratched his head. "You're taking this pretty calm, Mr. Burke."

"Why, thankee, Davey, never was one to lose my head. How about it, Home Run? You want to tell the boy, or should I?"

Hagerty, who looked well past retirement age at this point, couldn't answer.

"Guess I'll have to do it then. You see, Davey—" He leaned forward, the sharp point of his brown hair sliding forward over his forehead. "The truth is, I've known about this here business for a long time. Lot longer than you, I 'spect."

"You did?"

"Yep. You see, this Annie Gander woman—well, she contacted me first. Didn't even *think* of callin' on old Home Run here. No, sir. The way she figured it, the man who had the most to lose was poor old Cubby, the baby-food farmer. She figured that if people found out about little Donald kicking the bucket—well, that wouldn't sell much baby food, would it? Not that the food was responsible, of course, but you know the way people's minds work. So she came callin' on me, figuring I'd be able to support her in fine style. But she didn't know who she was dealin' with, no, sir." He chuckled.

Dave, who had expected to be the bearer of surprises, found himself the one surprised. If Annie had been blackmailing Burke, that explained Willie Shenk's recognition of the photograph . . .

"Yep, that Gander woman didn't faze me, Davey. If I had my druthers, I'da called the police and put her in jail. But considering the sitchyation, well, I said to her, if you want to make some spending money out of this, Miss Gander, why, you just go right down to see Homer Q. Hagerty, of Hagerty Tait Associates, 430 Madison Avenue. After all, my company puts seven million dollars' worth of commissionable advertising into his agency, and since *he's* the one who arranged this little hokey-pokey, why, I'm sure he'd be *glad* to take care of you. Eh, Home Run?"

"That's right," Hagerty said feebly. "That's absolutely right, Cubby. We made the mistake; we had to pay for it."

"Sure, that's how I looked at it. Like my gramps said, whoever dances to the tune gotta pay the piper. So you see, Davey boy, I don't exactly walk around blindfolded. No, siree. I know what's cookin' on the stove. I can smell it."

Dave looked at Hagerty for the first time.

"So I've been wasting my breath," he said bitterly. "You knew about it all the time, both of you. The least you could have done was tell me about it."

"Sure, that's what I say," Burke said jovially. "Let's give our team *all* the signals, Home Run. If Davey's gonna be on our side, let's not keep him in the dark." He flattened his floppy hands on the desk and stood up. "So let's forget hard feelings, huh? Let's have a good handshake all around and start fresh. What do you say?"

He stuck out his hand and Dave stared at it. Then, trancelike, he took and shook it. Burke did the same to Homer Hagerty, who accepted the handclasp glumly. The next handshake was the hardest. "Go on," Burke chuckled. "Go on, you two. Let's see a real old-fashioned glad hand."

Hagerty put out a limp bunch of fingers and Dave squeezed them gingerly.

"Shucks! You fellas can do better than that. After all, you boys *need* each other."

They looked at the floor and squeezed hands again.

"That's better," Kermit Burke said. "Now let's forget about it and get down to business. We're makin' progress, all right, but we can't get too smug about it. My gramps always said . . ."

They left Burke's office half an hour later. Neither spoke until they reached the street. Then Dave said:

"Did I hear you say I was fired?"

"Fired?" Hagerty said blankly. "What gave you that idea?"

"Just a notion."

"Wouldn't dream of it, Dave." He scowled. "I'm only sorry that you didn't come straight to me when you ran across the Gander story. I might have straightened things out, so we wouldn't have had to go through that business upstairs."

"I'm sorry. But things were getting complicated; you don't know *how* complicated."

"Here's a cab," Hagerty said.

In the back seat, Dave continued.

"Would it make things easier if I resigned?"

"Certainly not. You heard Burke; he likes you. And now that you're in on this switch business—well, I'd rather let things stand the way they are. Or does it bother you too much?"

"I'm not sure."

Dave looked out of the cab window onto the swift-moving view of Fifth Avenue. The warm weather had flushed out coveys of handsomely plumaged women. The stores were bright with merchandise. People walked briskly, with easy smiles for each other. It was a pleasant day, and not an unpleasant world.

"It's just not easy to forget about," Dave said, half to himself. "There's such a thing as integrity."

"It's a pretty word," Hagerty grunted.

"Yes, it is."

But he was thinking about another word.

"Murder," he said aloud.

"You're telling me," Homer Hagerty sighed, slumping into the seat. "This business is murder. How about having lunch with me? I know a place where you can drink the best lunches in town."

"You're the boss," Dave said.

XI. For Those Who Can Afford the Finest

The membership roster of the Mercantile Club listed one ex-President, one cabinet member, six senators, a dozen corporation heads, four elder statesmen of the motion pictures, and a hundred other names familiar to headlines and annual reports. Dave scanned the name plates while he waited for Homer Hagerty to check their coats, and felt suitably impressed. Hagerty returned, rubbing his palms together, and steered Dave into a carpeted room that was like Grand Central without an information booth.

Seated in leather armchairs around a marble-topped table, they waited until a white-coated patriarch responded to the ring of the hand bell. Hagerty ordered bourbon, and Dave asked for a whisky sour. Then the agency head, settling back and surveying the massive portraits on the walls, the winding marble staircase with its intricate black-iron railings, said: "What do you say, Dave? Like this place?"

"It has a kind of intimate charm."

"Wait'll you see the dining room upstairs. Took me four years to get elected to membership here; they're pretty particular. Costs two thousand a year to join, but it's worth it. You belong to any clubs, Dave?"

"I was once a member of the Aqua Velva After Shave Club, but I got thrown out for brawling."

Hagerty looked at him uncertainly, and then grinned. "Maybe you think this is an indulgence of mine, but it isn't. You meet a lot of important people here. In our business, it pays to join good clubs and eat in good restaurants. It's all part of the impression, and we're in a field where impressions count." He drummed on the table and stared ahead dreamily. "No, that's not strictly true. I didn't want to join the Mercantile for business reasons only. I wanted to join because it makes me feel good to be here."

"That sounds more like it," Dave said.

"Sure, why should I kid you? I like this kind of life, Dave. I like the fancy restaurants and the good whisky and all that stuff. I like having a Cad and a Jaguar and a big country house and a penthouse in the city. Don't underestimate these things, Dave, they've got a lot in their favor."

Dave laughed, with genuine delight. "I won't argue with you there, Mr. Hagerty."

"You betcha," Hagerty said, leaning forward, his face flushed. "I don't believe in all this meek and humble talk about the good life. Why the hell should I be ashamed of liking money? Ever since I was a kid in Pittsburgh, working in my father's ice house, I wanted to be able to afford all the luxury and high living I could get my hands on. Listen, the best thing that ever happened to the ad business was all

this talk about expense accounts and crack trains and beautiful models. That's what really attracts the young blood to
the agencies, don't kid yourself."

"I guess you're right."

"You're damn right I'm right!"

The drinks came, and Hagerty lifted his glass.

"There's nothing wrong with rich living," he said belligerently. "I like it, you like it, we all like it. Here's to your
health."

"To gout," Dave said. "My favorite disease."

They took the elevator to the upstairs dining room, two
drinks later. Hagerty's reserved table was set against a high
window overlooking Fifth Avenue. The food was superb.
Dave ate it slowly, and when he was done, continued to chew
on his lip.

"Still bothers you, doesn't it?" Hagerty said. "You can't
help thinking about the campaign?"

"It bothers me, all right. Look, I'm not passing moral
judgment on what you and Gordon did. In your shoes, I
might have done the same. But I feel about as comfortable
as a flagpole sitter with piles. The situation's too damn ex-
plosive."

"Is that all that's bothering you?" Hagerty breathed relief. "I can put your mind at ease fast, Dave. Just give me
the chance. I can show you that there's not a thing you'll
have to worry about except keeping Burke's kitty filled."

"You're more optimistic than I am. We've got half a
dozen people who know this precious secret. Any one of
them can blow the lid off."

"Sure. But none of them will, and I can prove it."

He unclipped a slim gold pencil from his inside coat

pocket, and picked up the Mercantile Club menu. He turned it around, and wrote busily for a full minute. Then he handed the card to Dave. It read:

> Homer Hagerty
> Kermit Burke
> Dave Robbins
> Janey Hagerty
> Irma and Howard Clarke
> Herbert Ruess
> Harlow Ross
> Countess Szylensca

"Let's check 'em off, Dave," he said, taking the menu back. "One by one. First of all, me."

"I'm not worried about you, Mr. Hagerty."

"Then let's cross me off."

He drew a line through the first name on the list.

"Then there's Kermit. You'll agree that we can eliminate him. And then there's you, Dave." He glanced up, grinned, and drew a line through the next two names.

"Then there's Janey," Hagerty said. "Maybe you think she'd like to see her old uncle in the breadline? I think we don't have to worry about Janey."

He crossed out the fourth name.

"As for the Clarkes, you said it yourself. They want that kid of theirs, and they're too scared to say anything. Ruess, in case you don't know the name, is the doctor who attended Donald during his trouble. You know his story. So let's cross out the next couple of lines."

He did.

"Then there's Harlow," Dave said uncomfortably. "He

gave the pictures to the Countess, so that means he knows. Don't ask me how."

"I know how," Hagerty said. "Harlow knows because he was in on it from the beginning."

"He was?"

"Of course," Hagerty chuckled. "Don't forget, Dave, before you came down the pike, Harlow was Gordon's assistant, and number one prospect for Gordon's job. It was Harlow who did all the detail work setting up the Burke campaign. And more important, it was Harlow more than anybody who screwed things up."

"You mean this was all Ross' fault?"

"Oh, I don't mean we don't share the responsibility. But it was Harlow's job to make all the technical arrangements with the couples we were going to photograph in the ads. He selected the Addisons and the Clarkes, and it was Harlow who set up the timing mechanism of the campaign. If he had been more careful, we wouldn't have started running the ads so soon after the baby's birth, and could have avoided the whole affair. As it is, if anybody gets a black eye for sloppy thinking, it's Harlow Ross. And don't think I won't use that information against him if he starts trouble. Ross knows that I can have him blacklisted with every agency in the country. No," Hagerty smiled, drawing two lines through Ross' name, "we won't have to be concerned about Harlow."

"That leaves the Countess," Dave said.

"Yes. And Kermit Burke holds the string that makes the Countess dance."

Hagerty crossed out the last name.

"Wait a minute," Dave said. "There's something else you

ought to know about the Countess. Burke's not the only one who's pulling strings. Mother Maggie's been doing a little tugging herself."

"How do you mean?"

"I didn't tell you what she was doing with those photos she got from Ross. She was using them to make *me* dance, to the tune of Here Comes the Bride."

Treading carefully, Dave told his boss about Sonya.

"Why, that's the damndest thing I ever heard," Hagerty said. "You really think she's trying to blackmail you into marriage?"

"That's what it amounts to. Not that Sonya is so unattractive. Or shy. Shy she's not. But the Countess still has some Old World ideas about picking and choosing her daughter's husband."

"Well, nothing to worry about now, is there? I mean, since Kermit knows the story, she can't do very much damage." He examined the troubled expression that still remained on Dave's face, and added: "But I'll tell you what. If it worries you any, I'll get Kermit to apply a little pressure. Maybe convince the Countess that the best thing for Sonya is a nice trip abroad."

"You think he could do that?" Dave's eyes brightened.

"I'm sure of it. We'll have Sonya aboard the *Ile de France* before the end of the month, you wait and see."

"Heaven help the crewmen," Dave murmured.

The waiter appeared, and Hagerty signed a chit.

"Let's go to my office and chew the fat a while," the president suggested. "There's something else I want to talk to you about."

He didn't describe the something else until they were back

at Hagerty Tait Associates. Even then, Dave didn't get the details until Hagerty buzzed his secretary and commanded the presence of Wilton Sheplow, the agency treasurer.

Sheplow came in with a brown accordion folder under his arm, peered at Dave suspiciously through his gleaming spectacles, and took a chair.

"Wilton," Hagerty said, "I wonder if you'd mind spelling out the agency position for Dave here."

Sheplow looked more dubious than ever, but undid the string around his file folder. He extracted a stapled sheaf of papers, and rattled the pages.

"You mean everything?" he said hollowly. "Confidential figures and everything?"

"Just a summary," Hagerty smiled. "Distribution of stock, net worth, that sort of thing. Stick to round figures."

Sheplow clicked his teeth.

"Hagerty Tait Associates was incorporated eight years ago with a capitalization of one hundred thousand dollars. The stock, consisting of a thousand shares, was divided equally between Mr. Hagerty and Mr. Tait. Presently, our liquid assets amount to approximately three hundred thousand dollars. These assets include cash in the bank, accounts receivable, a small inventory of art work amounting to seventy-five thousand, and a small remaining undepreciated value of furnishings and fixtures, about twenty-five thousand."

"The total was over four hundred thousand a few months ago," Hagerty said darkly. "But then we had that special business expense—"

"A hundred and twenty-five thousand," Sheplow said critically.

"Yes. But we're still worth good money, right?"

"Perfectly good money, Mr. Hagerty."

"And from our own forecasts, the value of our stock should increase considerably in the next couple of years. Right?"

"Speaking as treasurer—"

"Never mind. *I'm* telling you it'll increase. Now there's the question of Gordon's death. I don't know whether you realized this, Dave, but we never had a buy-or-sell agreement; Gordon had some kind of phobia against insurance. Figured he'd kick off the moment he paid his first premium; shows how wrong he was. So that means Mrs. Tait owns his half of the business. However, I've spoken to Grace about it, and she's agreed to sell the company half of that—twenty-five percent of the total. So that'll make two hundred and fifty shares of stock available for purchase."

"Book value, $312.47 a share," Sheplow said.

"Yes. Somebody's going to pick up that stock, Dave, and I want it to be you."

Dave crossed glances with Sheplow, and then with Hagerty. "You got the wrong pocketbook. I can't afford that kind of money."

"Who said anything about affording? I'm going to do the affording around here, Dave—I'm going to afford you an opportunity like you never had before. You know what a stock option is?"

"Not exactly."

"Well, it's very simple. I'm going to give you an option to buy that stock in the next two or three years, at its present book value. It's a sure thing that the stock will grow, so that without putting up a nickel, you can get a healthy chunk of capital-gains money. Now how does that sound to you?"

Sheplow made a strangled noise.

"You can go now, Wilton," Hagerty frowned. "Thank you very much."

The treasurer gathered his documents, tossed one incredulous look at the presidential desk, and left the office.

"Well, that's mighty generous of you, Mr. Hagerty—"

"Generous, crap. It's business for me, business and pleasure. For one thing, you've got Kermit's number. You're just the kind of sassy account man that Kermit will respect. For another, you're Janey's future husband."

"I wouldn't be so sure of that."

"Say, you think I don't know my Janey? Now I figured out what the problem was between you. It was all about the Burke Baby, wasn't it?"

"I guess so."

"Well, that's all straightened out now, isn't it? We understand each other now, don't we?"

"I suppose we do."

"Then we've eliminated that source of friction, haven't we?" Hagerty laughed. "It's wonderful what a little heart-to-heart talking will do, isn't it? Just think of all the problems we've licked today!" He stood up and thrust out his hand. "Now let's *really* shake hands, Dave. Let's have a real new beginning. What do you say?"

Dave grinned, and shook his hand.

"Okay with me, Mr. Hagerty."

"No more problems?"

"No, sir."

"No more deep dark secrets from now on?"

"No, sir."

"Attaboy. Now you get out of here and go to work; we

stockholders can't support a bunch of deadwood. But you might just take out a minute to speak to Janey; I think she'd like to hear from you."

"Okay, Mr. Hagerty," Dave said, smiling all over his face and going to the door.

"Oh, and Dave. Just one more thing."

"Yes, sir?"

"I don't think it's right for a major stockholder to be just anybody in the company, do you? I think we better make you a vice-president."

There was something beatific about Dave's expression as he went down the corridors of Hagerty Tait Associates. It was observed by the people he passed, and they gave him inquisitive nods of greeting without stopping to talk. Even when he entered Janey's office, and found it disappointingly empty, his face remained serene. He went back to his own quarters, and didn't mind when Louise reacted solicitously to his peculiar fixed smile.

"Are you all right, Mr. Robbins?"

"Of course I'm all right. Say, that's a mighty pretty dress you're wearing, Louise."

She looked stunned. "You really think so, Mr. Robbins?"

"I sure do. Like that color on you."

"Oh!" Louise said ecstatically, and attacked her type-writer furiously.

He shut his office door, slid into the swivel chair, and hoisted his feet to the desk. It was his first real experience with euphoria, and Dave floated on its soft, fluffy surface as if in a dream. After a few minutes of unthinking enjoyment, his mind began to work again, and he chuckled.

How could he have ever suspected Homer Hagerty of such a mundane crime as murder? The idea now appeared so ludicrous that it was laughable. Sure, Annie Gander had blackmailed Hagerty into a corner, and murder was a sure-fire method of eliminating blackmailers. But he had probably responded like all businessmen would to a threat to their net profit: with angry words, denunciations, a search for loopholes and alternatives, with bitterness and even hatred; then, finally, with payment on demand. The thought had never even entered his head, to conceal one crime with an even riskier crime. Dave tried to picture Homer Hagerty with a revolver bulging under his Brooks Brothers suit, and he chuckled again. He tried to visualize him face-to-face with Annie Gander, saying, in the steely voice of a movie-criminal: "Okay, sister, you asked for this . . ." And then yanking out the gun, thrusting its muzzle towards her. Bang! Bang! You're dead!

Dave swung his feet off the desk and clapped his hands on his knees. How could he have been so foolish? Murder wasn't committed by paunchy white-haired businessmen who spent their time between clubs, Cadillacs, cocktails, clients, and conference rooms. Murder was the occupation of wet-eyed men in overalls, of dirty-faced juveniles with switchblades in their pockets, of tight, menacing little men like Willie Shenk.

Willie Shenk. Of course it was Willie! The answer had been so simple and evident all the time, and he had denied it for its very simplicity. Willie had the opportunity, Willie had the means, and most important, Willie had the inclination. Yes, he had believed Shenk's story when he heard it in this very office; he had even felt stirrings of sympathy for the strange, narrow man with his protestations of affection for the dead woman. But Willie must be accustomed to slick denials of criminal deeds; it was part of his profession.

The morning newspaper was in Dave's wastebasket; he fished it out and skimmed through the back pages once more, looking for some mention of the Gander case. As usual, there was none. Why hadn't the police found Willie yet? If only he had been located and questioned—no, grilled was the word—maybe then the final answer would be forthcoming. He was almost tempted to call the police himself, and tell them about his rendezvous with Willie and Max Theringer. But he knew he couldn't.

Then he had a thought. Maybe Max could tell him something new; maybe some new evidence, some new police action had come to light . . .

He picked up the phone and called the *Times-Express.*

"Hello, Max? This is Dave Robbins. Just thought I'd call and see how you were."

"Dyspeptic," Theringer said. "How's Madison Avenue?"

"Same as ever. Say, how about you and me getting together soon? I could fill you in on my progress, and you can —well, how about tonight?"

"Won't have time tonight. Been doing a series on JD for the paper, got some copy to turn out. Never could work much after one of Gus' martinis."

"We don't have to go to Gus' place. I just want to chat. Suppose I came to your office after work?"

"Wouldn't exactly call it an office," Theringer said sourly. "I've got a desk and chair and private spittoon. But you're welcome to share the comforts, if you want."

"Fine, I'll be there around five-thirty."

"Make it six."

"Right," Dave said.

Janey didn't return for the rest of the afternoon, so there was no opportunity for Dave to extend the olive branch. At three-thirty, a staff memorandum was placed on his desk by the mailboy. It read:

It gives me pleasure to announce that Dave Robbins has been appointed a Vice President. I'm sure you will all want to congratulate Dave on the fine efforts which have earned him this title.

Homer Hagerty, Pres.

Dave put the memo into the bottom drawer of his desk, preserving it for posterity. Ten minutes later, Wilton Sheplow called and asked if he had a glossy photograph of himself for release to the newspapers and trade press. The rest of the afternoon was occupied by modest, grinning responses to the stream of Hagerty Tait employees who drifted in on congratulatory missions. Louise was the last to deliver her good wishes; she looked at her boss the way tourists look at the Lincoln Monument.

He left the office at five-thirty, and, encouraged by the balmy weather, walked across town to the *Times-Express* building. The directory told him that Max Theringer could be found on the fourth floor.

He walked between islands of cluttered desks, in an enormous room deserted by everyone except Max Theringer. The crime reporter was hunched over an ancient Remington like a hungry buzzard. He looked up at Dave's approach, but kept on hammering the keys with a blurring, two-finger motion. Dave pulled up a chair and waited until he whipped the page out of the roller.

"Well, what do you think of the place?" Theringer said, leaning back with a squeak of the chair. "Not exactly Lever House, is it? Well, what's on your mind, pal? You ever trace the connection between your friend Burke and Annie Gander? I've been wondering about that ever since."

"There's no real connection. Burke was the first blackmail victim Annie chose, that's all. That's why Willie saw him on the premises. But Burke was too cagey to shell out the money himself; he sent Annie to see Homer Hagerty, and he had to foot the bill. That's all there was to it."

"You sure about that?"

"Sure I'm sure. I've been doing a lot of thinking lately, and I came to the conclusion that maybe I went overboard. There's no question about the blackmail, but as far as murder goes—"

Theringer raised one of his skimpy eyebrows.

"What's this? Sound like you're singing a different tune, pal. Changed your mind about Hagerty?"

"It's not that I've changed my mind. I've never had any real evidence that Hagerty knocked off Annie, or made any of those attempts at my life. For that matter, I'm not so sure that any attempts *were* made. That railroad thing must have been an accident, and there never was any evidence of poison in that pill bottle. I'm beginning to think it's my lurid imagination, just like you thought at first."

The reporter slapped a pencil on the desk with a cracking sound. "You're a changeable cuss, ain't you? One day you're seeing bogymen on every corner, and now you're all sweetness and light. What the hell happened? Your boss give you a raise?"

Dave flushed. "It's not just that."

"So he did?"

"What if he did? It had nothing whatsoever to do with the murder; he doesn't even know I suspect him. But he's just not the murder *type*, if you know what I mean."

"No, I guess I don't. I've only been a crime reporter for about twenty years, and I never could find out what type commits murder. There was this nice old lady who taught nursery school, for instance. She chopped up her husband and sent the pieces to St. Louis. And there was this good-lookin' young lawyer, fresh out of college. He ran over his girl friend eight times with a Buick. And there was this minister—"

"Okay, okay," Dave said pettishly. "So maybe there isn't a murder type. But I ask you in plain English—isn't it a hell of a lot more likely that Willie Shenk bumped off Annie? Didn't he have the reason, the opportunity; wasn't he more the *type*?"

"Sure he was."

"Then do you believe his story? Do you think he's innocent?"

"That's the trouble with Willie. He's a good liar. So even if he tells the truth, you never know."

"But do you think he's innocent?"

"I don't *think* he's innocent," Max Theringer said. "I *know* he is."

Dave stiffened in the chair.

"What do you mean by that?"

"I talked to my friend Lieutenant Berger this morning.

They picked up Willie yesterday, and let him go four hours later. You see, the cops weren't actually fast asleep all this time, even if it looks that way. They've been checking every possible witness and every possible alibi since the murder took place. Not even Willie could establish his own innocence better than the police did. They didn't tell him this, of course, but he's no longer a real suspect."

The soft, fluffy cloud of Dave's euphoria was getting hard and bumpy.

"But what makes them so sure?"

"They talked to people in Annie's building. Two of them saw her—alive—three hours after Willie Shenk left the apartment. The clerk at the hotel Willie checked into was able to fix the time of his arrival. So was the bellhop. So was the bartender in the hotel saloon. There wasn't a detail of Willie's story that the police didn't know in advance. Crook or no crook, Willie Shenk didn't kill Annie Gander. And that, as you boys say, is how the cookie crumbles."

The narrow shoulders of Dave's suit appeared even narrower as he slumped in the chair.

"Then if Willie didn't do it . . ."

"Then somebody else did. Maybe somebody who really wasn't the killer type . . ."

Dave started another protest, but he was interrupted. The telephone on Theringer's desk jangled with startling volume. Dave jumped, but the reporter scooped up the receiver calmly and growled a salutation. He listened for a few minutes, said "Okay, thanks," and hung up. Then he folded his hands and looked at Dave inquiringly.

"You ever see a *real* murder?"

"What?"

"A real, honest-to-God murder. You've been talking and worrying about Annie's murder, but all you've really seen is a photograph and some newspaper stories. Maybe you're like most people about murder. They're so used to seeing 'em in the movies and on TV, reading about 'em in books—they start thinking maybe murder's an abstract thing, like some kind of game. But you ever see a real murdered corpse, without ketchup?"

"No," Dave said.

"Maybe you should. Maybe you ought to know what we're talking about when we use that word. Maybe you'll feel different." He nodded at the phone. "That was Berger. He's over on Fifteenth Street, in a rooming house. Some gal had her throat cut. Want to come along?"

Dave swallowed air. "You mean now?"

"Sure I mean now. I'm going over there, and I'm inviting you. I'll give you a press card so you can get in. You won't get many chances like this."

"All right," Dave said, standing up. "But I still want to talk about Annie."

"We'll talk later," Theringer said, hitching up the knot of his tie. "If you feel like talking."

In the street, Dave started to hail a cab, but Theringer muttered something about expense accounts and pulled Dave towards the subway kiosk on the corner. They rode underground in enforced silence until they reached the Fourteenth Street station, and came out into a shabbier world than the one they left. The rooming house was three blocks from the river, and there were four police cars and an official ambulance barricading that section of the neighborhood from the spectators. It had grown dark, and one of the police vehicles had a spotlight fixed on the building's entrance. It gave a curious, movie-set quality to the street.

Theringer used his press pass to enter the house, a dilapidated three-story brownstone. He greeted some of the officers and plain-clothes men familiarly, and Dave felt a sense of pride at being in his company. At the door of the murder victim's flat, a red-faced man in brown tweeds slapped Theringer's arm and looked at Dave with mild curiosity.

"This is Robbins," Theringer said. "He's a cub I'm training. Robbins, say hello to Lieutenant Berger."

Dave stuck out his hand; Berger looked perplexed, but took it. Then he opened the door, and they entered.

There were three men in the small room, one with a stethoscope trailing from his pocket. They were talking quietly together, in placid tones that gave Dave a sense of normality. They turned to them, and one even smiled at Theringer. Dave was calm and undisturbed. Why did Theringer look so grim?

Then he saw the body.

The girl must have been in her early twenties. Her clothes, an outsize wool sweater and an abbreviated skirt, had a junior-miss quality. There was something collegiate-cum-bohemian about her, with her short haircut, jagged across the forehead in Ondine fashion, her pert, retroussé nose, her pale pink lipstick. Her room was an extension of herself: college pennants shared the walls with Braque prints. She must have read a great deal, too; the bookshelves had a self-installed look, and they were crowded in a kind of disarray that indicated usage. She looked like a rather charming, sweet, thoughtful, interesting girl; Dave thought he probably would have liked her.

Then, in the terrible second moment of his appraisal, the shock of the truth stunned him with painful impact. She was none of these things. All that was past, ended abruptly in a tick of the clock and the sweep of a knife blade. Now she was a *thing*, sprawled grotesquely across a hooked rug that had greedily soaked the blood she had lost. The long supple legs were twisted at a shameless angle, the eyes were shut, the mouth was gaping, and below the mouth—

Dave nearly retched, and Theringer, spotting his reaction in time, shoved him out of the doorway into the hall. Lieutenant Berger, talking to a patrolman outside, looked at them questioningly, but was understanding enough not to smile at Dave's plight.

Theringer held his arms as they went down the stairs and out into the restorative coolness of the street.

"I feel so stupid," Dave said. "It was just the shock. That wound—"

"Almost slashed her head off," Theringer grunted. "Pretty little kid, too."

"But what kind of fiend—"

"How the hell should I know?" Theringer said roughly. "Any kind of fiend. Boy friend, maybe, or the janitor, or some friend who hated her good looks, or maybe some degenerate who wandered into the building—who can say? How do you spot a killer?" His voice softened when he saw Dave's color. "Look, pal, you're all shook up. How about a drink?"

"Good idea. There's a place on Sixteenth Street, called Ferdy's—"

"Tell you what. You go there and get yourself a nice warm

shot, and I'll go back and do my job upstairs. I'll meet you there in fifteen minutes, maybe less. Okay?"

"Okay," Dave said.

It was twenty minutes before Theringer found Dave in the booth at Ferdy's, still nursing his first drink.

When Theringer sat down, he sighed heavily and said: "Short-short story. Kid from the grocery confessed to the slaying an hour after they found the body. Nice-looking boy, kind of the neighborhood Lothario. Must have made a pass at her and she got excited, screamed, something like that. He got scared, lost his head, and—"

"Terrible," Dave said. "To do a thing like that—"

"He was scared," Theringer snapped. "When people get scared, they do funny things. All he was scared about was getting locked up on a rape charge. Other people get scared for different reasons. You threaten to take away a guy's livelihood, his prestige, everything that's important to him—he'll get scared, and sometimes desperate. Desperate enough to kill."

Dave knew what he meant.

"All right. So what you're saying is that murder's a pretty rotten business, and it doesn't matter why it gets committed—"

"Something like that."

"And you think I'm wrong about Homer Hagerty. You think my original suspicion was right."

"That's up to you. Like you said, there's not much evidence."

Dave thumped the table, making Theringer's highball

glass rhumba. "That's what I mean. There's no evidence; just suspicion. Even if I wanted to prove it—"

"That's not your job, pal. That's what the police get salaries for. All you've got to do is tell them what you know, and let them look for corroborating facts."

"But I can't make an accusation like that! It would—" He stopped.

"It would louse things up for you, wouldn't it? With that fancy job of yours, and that girl."

Dave squirmed miserably.

"What would *you* do in my shoes, Max?"

"Who, me?" The reporter chuckled dryly. "Me, I'd collect my check every week, live off the expense account, drive a Cadillac, drink my martinis like a good boy, marry the girl, buy me a house in Connecticut, and forget the whole business. That's what *I'd* do. But then I'm a rotten, no-good son of a bitch."

Dave finished the rest of his drink in a gulp.

"All right. I want to do the right thing, Max. But if there's some way I can keep the police out until I'm sure—"

Theringer drummed the table.

"Well, there's one way. But it's not the easiest thing in the world."

"What's that?"

"This kind of crime we're dealing with—it's a crime that breeds crime, if you know what I mean. Annie commits blackmail, the blackmail leads to murder. You find out too much about the murder—somebody tries to knock you off. It's a chain reaction."

Dave thought of Bob Bernstein, but held his tongue.

"As long as there's a threat to the murderer's existence,"

Theringer said, "he'll probably go on committing murder. And if he thought there was somebody who constituted as great a threat as Annie Gander was—there might be another murder attempt. Right?"

"I don't know."

"Want to find out?"

"How do you mean?"

"Come on, don't be dense. You think your boss is too nice a type to kill, why not prove it once and for all? Give him somebody else to worry about, somebody he'll want to get rid of even more than he did Annie Gander. I'm talking about bait, pal, you know what bait is?"

"Wait a minute. If you're thinking of me—"

"As a matter of fact, I wasn't. You would have been nice, fresh bait once, but now you've begun to smell a little. No, I wasn't thinking of you, Davey. I was thinking about Willie."

"Willie Shenk?"

"That's right. I was just wondering how your boss would react to Willie. He must know about him, if he knows anything about Annie. And if Willie decided to take up where Annie left off . . ."

Dave did a double-take worthy of Edward Everett Horton.

"Let me get this straight. You mean we sick Willie Shenk on Hagerty as another blackmailer? And wait for him to knock Willie off?"

"Sure, who'd miss Willie? He's just a dirty smudge on the police blotter." Theringer scowled and smiled at the same time. "No, I don't mean exactly that. I mean we give Hagerty every opportunity to take care of Willie the same way he took care of Annie—at least in my opinion. The only difference is, we arrange things so that it never gets that far. Then we'll have more evidence than we need to hang him."

"But why would Willie co-operate? And what if something went wrong?"

"I can't answer either question. I *think* Willie'd co-operate, because he doesn't know he's off the suspect list, and I might be able to convince him that it's the only way to clear himself of a murder charge. I *think* it won't go wrong if we take the right precautions. But I can't promise anything. When you go fishing for sharks, even with good bait, sometimes the shark gets you."

"I don't like it," Dave said uneasily.

"I don't blame you. But it's one way to settle your mind about your boss' guilt or innocence. It's up to you, pal. Like I said, you can just take the cash in hand and waive the rest. That's the sensible thing to do."

Dave stared into his drink, as if looking for an answer in the bobbing ice.

"If you really think Willie will play along . . ."

"That's my guess."

"Then so will I," Dave said.

When he reached his apartment later that night, all the light switches Dave could flick to "on" position didn't serve to vanquish the gloom.

It was ten o'clock, and he wasn't sleepy. He turned on the television set and watched a broken-hearted quiz show contestant drive off in a glistening white Cadillac. There was a vintage crime movie on the Late Show, and he followed its blood-drenched plot with much too much empathy. At a commercial break, he decided not to listen to what doctors recommend for pains of headache, neuralgia, and arthritis, and went into the kitchen for a bottle of ale. The telephone was ringing when he returned, and he picked it up.

"Dave? You weren't asleep, were you?"

"No. Who's this?"

The woman said: "Ruth Bernstein. I tried to call you before, but you weren't home. Listen, I've been thinking about what you said when you were here, and it's been bothering me. Why was it so important, to know who came here for a portrait?"

Dave closed his eyes. "It's really not that important, Ruth. I was just curious."

"Well, you got me worried. I'd hate to tell you the *thoughts* I had. Did you have those pictures developed?"

"Yes. But the camera must have opened during the explosion; all the film was exposed."

"That's too bad. Anyway, I did some investigating today, just to see if I could find anything at all among Bob's papers and stuff. I thought if you were still interested in knowing—"

"Of course I am!"

"Well, I found an old ledger that Bob used to use sometimes, for making notes, taking down phone numbers, things like that. It was in the desk, right in the front hall. Most obvious place in the world."

"Yes?" Dave said, controlling his anxiety.

"It's not what you could call an appointment book or anything, but it must have been up to date. Under September six, for instance"—her voice went fuzzy—"he had a note to himself about our anniversary, a little reminder. And on the date of his death, he had a name written on the page. It must have been the person who came out for the portrait."

"Who was it?" Dave said lightly, detached and almost uninterested.

"I've got the book in front of me. It says 'F—Janey Hagerty.' I don't know what the 'F' means, but you know Janey Hagerty, don't you? That nice girl who works at your agency? Dave?"

XII. It's Shot from Guns

Tuesday was the worst day. Tuesday didn't have the numbing effect of Monday, the middle-of-the-week solidity of Wednesday, the hopeful face of Thursday, the home-stretch feel of Friday. Tuesday was the worst, and Dave woke in a tangle of steamy sheets to the idea that this Tuesday would cap them all.

For the first time in weeks, he decided to fortify himself with a normal-sized breakfast. Throughout its preparation, his mind revolved around the thought of Janey.

What was her name doing on Bernstein's calendar? Had she been the client who made the portrait appointment? Yet on the day of the photographer's fatal accident, Janey had accompanied Dave to the Clarkes' home in the suburbs; she hadn't left his side for a moment. If she had made the appointment for herself, why hadn't she kept it? And if she had made it for someone else . . .

He burned a finger cracking open a soft-boiled egg and howled. The toast popped out underdone; he replaced it and got himself a black, inedible cinder. The coffee was watery, and he couldn't get the cap off the marmalade jar.

Still hungry, he left the house. A light drizzle had evaporated the available taxis, so he caught a cross-town bus. Its slow progress tormented him; there were so many questions crowding his mind that he was anxious to face Janey and learn the answers. If she had made the appointment for Uncle Homer, why didn't she mention the fact? Was the omission deliberate? And what did the "F" beside her name stand for?

But when he reached the office, he found Janey's room empty.

Jody, the receptionist, answered his question.

"Miss Hagerty? She's home in bed. Started to have the sniffles yesterday afternoon, and left around two."

"Thanks," Dave said "I'll call her there "

He did, from the telephone at his own desk, and when Janey answered, it was in a clogged, miserable voice.

"Gee, I'm sorry to hear you're sick," Dave said. "Is there anything I can do?"

"You cad leab me alode," Janey said testily "I was soud asleeb when you called."

"I wouldn't bother you, except that something important came up. I went out to see Mrs. Bernstein. Bob's wife."

"Did you pudge her in de doze?"

"What's that?"

"I thought that was your dew hobby, pudging people in de doze."

"Don't be funny. Ruth told me that somebody made an

appointment for a portrait sitting the day Bob was killed. She didn't know who when I saw her, but last night she called me again. She said she found your name on his calendar."

"My *dame?*"

"Yes. Did you make the appointment?"

"I did dothing of the kind," Janey said. "Now will you blease go 'way and let me sleeb?"

"Did you make the appointment for somebody else?"

"I *told* people that Bob took portraits, to help him out when he lost the Burke job. But *I* didn't make any appointment. Now leab me alode or I'll blow virus germs right through the telephode."

"Okay, okay," Dave frowned, "I'll leab you alode. But I want to see you, Janey; I've got so much to tell you . . ."

"Haven't you learned how to say bye-bye yet?"

"Okay, okay. Goodbye."

A few minutes later, the head of the Media department came in to discuss forthcoming Burke schedules. He spent the next hour in a tedious discussion of rates and discounts and merchandising support. The media man was still in his office at eleven, when Louise picked up his ringing telephone, and announced:

"Mr. Theringer wants to speak to you."

"Hold him on the phone," Dave said. "We all through, Jerry? This is a kind of personal call."

"Sure, we're through."

Dave snatched up the receiver when he was alone, and whispered: "Max? What's happening?"

"Plenty. I got hold of our mutual friend last night, the one with the funny nose. I thought I'd have to give him a big argument about what we talked about, but I was wrong. He jumped at the idea."

"He did?"

"I guess Willie's reforming," Theringer chuckled. "He's just as anxious to solve the case as the cops are. I told him the details of the plan, and got him to draft a letter to you-know-who, in his own inimitable handwriting. It was hand-delivered this morning, so it must be on his desk right now."

"Right now?" Dave gulped, looking at the doorway as if expecting to see Homer Hagerty's wrathful figure.

"Yep. I think we ought to get together as soon as possible, so you can see the letter and hear the details of the plan. You free for lunch?"

"Yes. Listen, can we make it uptown? At LeVal's on Fifty-eighth Street?"

"Sure, if you're buying."

"I'm buying," Dave said.

They met at twelve-fifteen, under the canopy of the restaurant. Theringer gave black looks to everyone associated with the posh enterprise; he scowled at the doorman and pushed the door himself. He glared at the checkroom girl, grumbled at the head waiter, and snapped at the busboy who tried to fill his bread plate with delicate strips of cornbread.

"What a joint," he said disgustedly.

"You don't like it?"

"I love it, that's the trouble. I can't afford it, so I gotta hate it. But let's get down to business."

He reached into his pocket for a folded sheet of paper, and handed it across the tablecloth.

"This is the letter I wrote for Willie. He didn't write it

exactly this way; he improved the English a little. But it's essentially the message your boy Hagerty got this morning."

Dave read it.

Hagerty—

I know all about youse and Annie Gander. Annie was my girl. I seen the pictures of that baby you been using in the Burke ads, and that's my kid. I know where you got him and I don't like what you done to Annie. If you don't want no trouble from me, you better get a hundred grand ready for me by tonight. If you don't come across I'll tell the cops what I know. I mean this. I'll be waiting for you at nine o'clock at the Westmore Arms Hotel on Forty-first Street and Eighth Avenue, Room 208. Better be there if you know what's good for you.

(signed)
Willie Shenk

"Like I said," Theringer chuckled, "Willie thought it was okay except for the English. He was very offended at the style."

"And Hagerty's seen this?"

"If he looked at his morning mail, he saw it. Willie delivered it in person at nine o'clock. His secretary took it. Just in case Hagerty has any doubts as to its authenticity, he can just ask his gal. She'll describe Willie, all right."

"This Westmore Arms Hotel. There really is such a place?"

"Of course. It's a cheap residential joint right across the street from the City Room bar; I checked Willie into his room last night. I figured if we had to make a stakeout, we might as well be comfortable. We'll get a fine view of the building entrance from Gus' window. All we got to do is hang around until we see Hagerty enter. If he shows up."

"You think maybe he won't?"

"Your guess is as good as mine. But if he does—we go up after him."

"What if we're too late? What if he—"

"Don't fret about Willie; he can handle himself. Your boss may be pretty hot stuff for an amateur, but Willie's a pro." A waiter slipped a steak under Theringer's nose, and he squinted at it disparagingly. "Looks awful," he said. "I'm sure to hate it."

"You mean that's all there is to it?" Dave said. "Just you and me in the City Room, waiting for Hagerty to show up?"

"What'd you expect? The FBI? Gang Busters?"

"No, but—"

"I know what's bothering you, but forget it. I've got Lieutenant Berger alerted to stand by for trouble tonight. I didn't tell him what kind of trouble, but he'll be waiting for my call as soon as anything develops. So relax."

"I dunno. It sounds simple enough, but—"

"I said take it easy. Just go back to work and act like nothing's happened. That's all you've got to worry about. Boy, this steak is lousy," Theringer said, wolfing it down.

Theringer's injunction wasn't easy to follow. By two-thirty, Dave had smoked half an inch from every cigarette in his pack. Louise came in and clucked at the sight of his ashtray.

"Celia called while you were out, Mr. Robbins. Mr. Hagerty was looking for you."

"He was?" He picked up the phone and called the president's office.

Celia said: "Well, he's gone now, Mr. Robbins. He and Mr. Sheplow had to go to the bank or some place, but he said he would be back around three-thirty."

He stared at the receiver after replacing it. The bank! Did that mean he was obeying Willie's instructions?

He bought another pack of cigarettes at the machine in the hallway, and filled another ashtray. At four, Louise brought him the message: Hagerty had returned, and wanted to see him.

He walked into the president's office and saw an old, enfeebled man in Hagerty's leather swivel chair. He seemed to be having difficulty breathing; his collar was loosened around a parchment-dry throat, and his lips were blue.

"Hello, Dave," he croaked. "Have a seat."

Dave sat down, eyes glued to the altered features of Uncle Homer.

"Something I want to talk to you about," Hagerty said, every word an effort. "I'm not feeling so hot, Dave, not so hot at all. This whole Burke affair is taking too much out of me. It's not worth it, you know; look at Gordon . . ."

"You ought to take it easier, Mr. Hagerty."

"Yes, that's what I think. Take it easier. This baby campaign, for instance. Hell, it's just a lousy ad campaign, that's all. The world wouldn't come to an end if we discontinued it, right?"

"Right."

"It's too full of pitfalls, that's what it is. You said it yourself, yesterday. It's like sitting on dynamite; you never know when somebody'll kick you where it counts. I've been thinking about it a lot, and I figure the best thing to do is drop it."

"The Burke Baby?"

"Yes, the goddam Burke Baby. I never want to hear about that brat again. I'm going to call Kermit tomorrow and tell him what I think. Oh, he'll scream bloody murder, all right; he likes the way that sales curve looks. But I think I can convince him that it's not the only campaign in the world. And if he wants to make trouble—well," Hagerty said darkly, "I can be pretty tough in a fight."

Dave whistled unmusically.

"That's quite a surprise, Mr. Hagerty. After everything you said yesterday."

"Most of it still goes, Dave. You're still getting that stock option, don't worry about that. We may have to make some adjustments; had some unexpected expenses recently. But I'll make it up to you, Dave, I promise you that."

Dave waited for more, but Hagerty seemed to have concluded. He stood up and went to the door.

"That all, Mr. Hagerty?"

The president opened his mouth, then shut it again, nodding affirmatively.

Then: "Dave!"

"Yes, sir?"

"Better talk to Joe Spiegel about getting some new copy thinking started. We'll need a new campaign—and a damn good one—just about as fast as he can whip it up. All right?"

"Right, Mr. Hagerty."

He found Spiegel doing a Double-Crostic, his glasses teetering at the end of his nose. Spiegel wouldn't even talk to him until he had found an eight-letter word meaning Variety of Turtle. When Dave supplied him with "terrapin," he snapped his suspenders and let Dave deliver his message.

"New campaign?" the copy chief said in disbelief. "What the hell for?"

"Some day I'll tell you all about it. The main thing is, Hagerty's out of love with little Donald."

"Then let's find another kid."

"That's a good solution. But this Burke Baby's not even six months old; we don't have any excuse for switching kids so soon. Hey, wait a minute." Dave snapped his fingers. "What if we *did* stop this series and begin a new one—but for a reason?"

"What reason?"

"Why not make a national contest out of the Burke Baby? Then we can explain why we stopped the campaign—that we were just running a teaser before the *real* series began. It's a little thin, sure—"

"What kind of contest are you talking about?"

"A big whoop-te-doo, you know what I mean. Only young couples having their first baby can enter. It's all designed to select the *new* Burke Baby, get it? We can give away lots of prizes, but the biggest prize of all is appearance in the Burke Baby Food ads. We can do it every year, just this way. Should have great merchandising possibilities—"

Spiegel looked unhappy.

"You want to take the bread out of my mouth? I'm supposed to have the ideas around here."

"You don't like it?"

"I do, damn it. I think it'll work."

"Then will you turn something out for me? A memo, maybe a sample ad?"

"How soon?"

"You mean you haven't done it yet?" Dave blinked. Then he laughed, snapped Spiegel's suspender in a sudden outburst of good humor, and left the office.

But his high spirits took a rapid descent a few minutes later. There was still tonight to look forward to, an opportunity to be star witness to a murder.

He was too restless to stay in his own office. He wandered out aimlessly, but with a purposeful stride. He stopped at Janey's empty office and examined the display on her bulletin board: tear sheets of esthetic advertisements that had pleased her art director's eye; high-key photos from the photographers' sample books; a Picasso print torn from the pages of *Art Annual*. He felt a stirring of affection; not just for Janey, but for all the artists who brought their talents to the agencies, the brash and often inarticulate people who tried to bring beauty into a commercial world, and were the first to leer and scoff if they were accused of it.

He passed the tiny cages of the copy writers, the shy, self-appointed elite, who felt more pride than they would admit to in the products of their cerebration. He passed a cubicle containing the agency's only radio-TV expert, a harried young man who read *Variety* and talked about show biz and whose carnival manner sometimes obscured the fact that he knew precisely what he was doing. He passed the research department, and caught the murmured words of an academic argument about depth interviewing. All along the route, he saw the worried faces of the account executives, suffering their peculiar martyrdom of being bullied by their clients and misunderstood by their associates. Suddenly,

Dave thought he liked the advertising business. It wasn't pleasant to realize that his career might end tonight.

He completed his tour of the office and went back to his own desk. He remained there until six, and went out to a lonely dinner at a moderate-priced restaurant.

At eight o'clock, he kept his date with Max Theringer.

He was at the bar, staging a one-sided argument with Gus. When he saw Dave, the reporter grinned and made room for him at the adjoining stool.

"All set?" Theringer asked.

"I guess so. Where's this hotel that Willie's at?"

Theringer nodded at the plate glass with the gold-embossed legend: мооя утіɔ. Across the street, a frayed green canopy flapped in the breeze over a five-step stoop. The faded letters spelled out: westmore arms hotel— *Permanent and Transient.* Dave counted its six stories.

"It's the perfect place," Theringer said. "We can't miss seeing anybody enter from here. All we've got to do is be patient." He squinted at Dave. "What's the matter, pal? You look sick."

"I feel sick. I'm not so sure this is a good idea."

"I'm willing to hear a better one. What's your complaint? Think Hagerty won't show up?"

"No, I think he will. He went out early this afternoon with Sheplow, the agency treasurer. His secretary thought he went to the bank."

"So what's wrong with that? If he makes the payment, that doesn't mean he's a murderer. Matter of fact, it might indicate he's innocent."

"That's what I mean," Dave said forcibly. "If he gives Willie the money, it won't prove anything either way. He might be willing to pay to keep Willie quiet, without knowing anything about the murder. On the other hand, he might be the killer, and hasn't enough nerve left to take care of Willie, too. You said so yourself. Annie was just a foxy dame; Willie's a professional hood."

"But if he *does* try and take care of Willie—would that be proof enough?"

"I guess so," Dave said miserably. "Give me a beer, Gus."

The tavern had a lazy clock. Its minute hand moved imperceptibly around the circle of numbers. They watched in silence, Dave inwardly cursing its lack of speed.

At eight-thirty, he said: "You sure this Lieutenant Berger's standing by? Sure he took you seriously?"

"Positive. He'll be on the spot five minutes after I place the call. So stop worrying."

Twenty minutes later, it was eight thirty-five.

"Not a soul's gone into the place," Dave said. "They don't do a rushing business, do they?"

"It's not exactly the Waldorf," Theringer said. "How about another beer?"

"No, thanks."

Ten minutes later, Dave said: "I'll have a Canadian Club. Neat."

Then it was nine o'clock.

"No sign of him yet," Theringer grunted.

"Maybe he chickened out—"

"Or maybe he's just late. You ad boys don't dote on punctuality, do you? What time do you get to the office?"

"Nine-thirty, ten."

"See what I mean?"

At five minutes past the hour, an old woman with an umbrella went up the steps of the Westmore Arms.

"This is terrible," Dave said. "My ulcers are getting ulcers—"

"Shut up and keep looking."

They kept looking, and the tavern clock over the mirror took on a burst of speed. It became nine-ten with alarming swiftness.

"I don't like this," Theringer growled. "Guilty or innocent, Hagerty should have kept that appointment. He'd be too scared not to."

"Is there any other way into the hotel?"

"There's a rear exit in the alley, but he wouldn't know about that. Maybe something's happened to him Or maybe—"

Theringer slammed his beer glass on the bar.

"What's the matter?"

"I just had a horrible thought," the reporter said. "If I'm right, then we've *really* loused things up—"

"What are you talking about?"

Theringer swept a raincoat from the rack. "Come on. We're going to see Willie."

"Now? But what if Hagerty shows up? What if he sees me?"

"We'll have to take the chance. Come on!"

He followed Theringer out of the bar, bleating his complaints. The older man moved like an athlete, broken-field running through the traffic as they crossed the street. He took the steps of the Westmore Arms in two jumps, and raced through the seedy lobby of the hotel without waiting for Dave to keep pace.

"Never mind the elevator," he growled. "We'll take the stairs."

Dave was so winded by the time they reached the second floor that he fell against the wall and panted like an overheated poodle. Theringer rapped sharply against the door of Room 208.

There wasn't any answer.

"Oh, my God," Dave said, "you don't think he's—"

"I don't know." Theringer turned the knob. It yielded, and the door opened.

Dave braced himself for the sight of another corpse. All he saw was a linoleum floor, an iron bed with a sagging bedspread, a metal bureau, and a peeling white chair.

"It's empty!"

"Brilliant," Theringer said acidly.

"Are you sure he was here?"

"I left him lying on that bed at seven-thirty." He went over to the bed and looked at the rumpled covers. There was a true-crime magazine on the floor, alongside an ashtray crammed with tiny butts. "Maybe he got cold feet and took a powder. Or maybe it's something else—"

"You mean he sneaked out on us?"

"Maybe worse than that. Maybe I was taking too much for granted about Willie's reformation. This may be a double-cross."

"What kind of double-cross?"

"I thought Willie really wanted to co-operate. When I told him about the plan, he was as eager as all hell. But maybe he wasn't thinking about trapping Annie's murderer —maybe he was thinking about that hundred grand."

"Then why didn't he wait for Hagerty?"

"Because he couldn't, you sap. He knew we were parked across the street, that we had Lieutenant Berger waiting for a call. He couldn't get away with the dough here. But if he changed the place of rendezvous—"

Dave had to sit down.

"I know, I know," Theringer said gloomily. "It's all my fault for being so damn smug about Willie. I never even thought of the possibility. But you can see how tempting it was—"

"What'll we do?"

"Don't ask me. I suppose we can get Berger to put out a police call for Willie. But by the time they find him, it may be too late. Either he'll get away with the money, or your pal Hagerty will—"

"We've got to find them!" Dave said. "If we don't—" Inspiration hit him. "Wait a minute. Celia!"

"Who?"

"If Willie changed the place of rendezvous, then he must have called the office today. Hagerty's secretary could have taken the message; she'll know where they are!"

"It's worth a try."

Dave picked up the telephone on the night table, and then replaced it. "What the hell am I doing? I don't even know her home number." He slid the Manhattan directory onto his lap and stared at the cover blankly. "Celia Clancy? Celia Comstock? Celia Carrington?"

"What are you doing?"

"I can't remember her last name!"

"Oh, fine."

"I *know* her name, damn it. I just can't think of it."

"You ought to take a memory course."

"I did, once."

"Too bad you forgot it."

"It's no use." He shoved the book back into the drawer of the night table. "I've worked with her almost two years, but I just don't know her last name."

"Then I guess we've had it," Theringer sighed.

"There's only one other thing I can think of," Dave said. "It's a small chance, but maybe the only one. If we went to Hagerty's office, we might find a note or something on his desk. Maybe he wrote down the new address Willie gave him."

Theringer rubbed his chin.

"Not a bad idea," he said admiringly. "You're getting shrewd at this business, Robbins."

The compliment pleased him, but Dave said gruffly:

"Let's get going."

When they spilled out of the cab in front of the Hagerty Tait building, Dave's eyes traveled up the steel-and-glass expanse, searching for lights on the thirteenth floor.

"Can't tell if anyone's up there," he said.

"Cleaning women maybe?"

"No, they finish the floor around seven-thirty. We'll ask the night man."

The night man, a bitter redhead in grimy overalls, said:

"Yep. Fella went up there around nine o'clock."

Dave and Theringer looked at each other.

"Did he sign the book?"

"*Everybody* gotta sign the book," the man said, spinning it towards them.

Dave peered at the last entry.

It read: *Homer Hagerty—13th Floor.*

"They're here!" Dave gasped.

"Nope," the redhead said. "Only one fella up there. You goin' upstairs?"

"You bet we are," Theringer said grimly.

Dave scratched his name on the ledger and then raced for the automatic elevator with Theringer at his heels. He stabbed his finger on the button, and paced the tiny floor impatiently until the doors slid open again on the thirteenth floor.

They walked out of the car into the Early American lobby, lit eerily by the glow of the green lantern on the reception desk. The glass doors leading to the inner offices were closed, and Dave jangled a bunch of keys out of his pocket. It took him three tries to find the right one.

"Think we're too late?" he said.

"I don't think anything. Let's go in."

Dave halted on the other side of the doors, squinting down the darkened corridor.

"Is there a light switch for the hall?" Theringer said.

"Some place, but I'll be damned if I know where. Hagerty's office is at the end of the corridor. Think you can make it in the dark?"

"I'm no owl," Theringer muttered. "But go ahead."

They tiptoed, noiseless as Indians on a raid, except that Theringer's shoes had developed a comic squeal, and Dave banged a knee against the water cooler outside of Hagerty's office.

"Door locked?" Theringer whispered.

Dave turned the knob slowly, and was relieved to hear the click of the latch.

"No."

He opened the door. He fumbled around the inside wall for the switch plate, but couldn't find it. The Venetian blinds were drawn against the three windows of the office, but thin slices of moonlight filtered through and cast blue-white stripes over the carpeting.

"Can't see a damn," Theringer grumbled.

Dave finally located the switch. He flicked it down, and the egg-crated fluorescents overhead blinked once, twice, and then brought daylight into the room.

The office appeared normal. There was a green leather couch. A credenza containing an unused library of books and an often-used library of liquor bottles. An antiqued table with bowlegs and an inlaid mother-of-pearl surface. A massive mahogany desk, neat and polished to a high gloss.

Then Dave realized what was missing.

"The chair!" he said

There was no swivel chair visible behind the desk. Dave stepped closer and saw that it had fallen to the carpet, brought down by the bloodied hand that had clutched its leather arm for support. The body was lying embryo-fashion beside it, as if doubled up with the pain of the stomach wounds which had eventually brought death. The splash of blood on the white shirtfront, the frozen attitude of agony, made Dave retch and spin about to avoid the sight. Theringer, less sensitive, dropped to his knees and made a hasty inspection of the corpse. By the time he got to his feet, Dave was out of the office and bent low over the water-cooler spout, filling his mouth with the icy stuff and gasping for breath.

"Take it easy," the reporter said. "You should be used to this."

"I don't want to get used to it. Who . . ."

"Willie," Theringer answered grimly. "It's poor Willie Shenk. This was the new rendezvous place. Everything came off just as we thought, except we made it too late . . ."

"We should call the police—"

"Not in Hagerty's office; we don't want to touch anything in there. Where can I find a phone?"

"There's another night line, in Sheplow's office. Right down the hall."

He started for it, but Theringer's hand closed around his elbow and halted him.

"Wait a minute."

"What is it?"

"Am I crazy, or did I hear something moving?"

Dave paused, and listened so hard that his ears began to ring.

"I don't hear anything."

"What's on that side of the floor?"

"More offices, of course. Say, what's eating you?"

"Nothing. I just think we ought to be careful, that's all."

"Careful? I'm sick of being careful! And I'm sick of playing Dick Tracy, too! From now on, the police can handle this whole mess. That's what they get paid for."

He shook off the reporter's hand and went striding down the hallway towards the treasurer's office. He turned in the doorway, ducked his left hand inside and snapped on the light switch. When the bright glare filled the room, he blinked, but the sudden blur of motion in the corner of the office evoked an even more violent reaction. He yelped in surprise when he realized that Sheplow's office wasn't empty, and when its frightened occupant raised a quivering arm to point the gun's muzzle at his chest, he yowled in rage and sprang forward. It wasn't until ten minutes later that he knew he had been shot, and he laughed giddily when Theringer told him. Two wars hadn't left him with a single bullet wound, and there he was, bleeding in his gray flannel suit.

XIII. Compare and You'll See Why

"We should have *realized*," Janey said, holding a Kleenex to her pink nose. "From the minute we knew about the baby switch, we should have figured it out."

Dave, looking gallant and distinguished with the white sling on his left arm, reached over and took her free hand. Janey was propped up in bed, the night table beside her laden with cold remedies and sickroom supplies. The only thing healthy about her was her curiosity.

"Don't upset yourself about it," he said gently. "We'll talk about it when you're feeling better."

"Don't you dare," she said hotly. "I want to talk about it *now*. When I think what lousy detectives we were—"

"Oh, I dunno," Dave said defensively. "I didn't do so bad, considering everything."

"But we should have known that there was something

fishy about that baby. Where would Gordon *find* a baby so readily to replace little Donald? It takes months, *years* to get one from an adoption home, and you can't just *advertise* for an infant that age. I don't care *how* good an ad man you are."

"Remember the day of the shooting at the Clarkes' house? You said there was something familiar about the kid."

"Yes, but I still didn't know what. Something about the eyes and the nose . . . But I just didn't connect the face with Gordon. Even if I had, I would have thought it was just a coincidence. I didn't think Gordon was the type who would—well, you know."

"Oh, he was the type, all right. Gordon knew Annie Gander long before the Burke campaign. He'd been paying the rent on that hotel suite of Annie's for over sixteen months. And when Annie produced her little surprise package, he footed all the medical expenses. So you can see what went through his mind when little Donald died. He knew just the baby to put into the Clarke cradle—his own. He knew the mother wouldn't mind parting with it, for a suitable fee. And he wouldn't mind being rid of it himself."

"How awful," Janey said. "The poor little thing . . ."

"I wouldn't worry about him; the Clarkes will love him like their own. Maybe he came out luckiest in this business."

"The one I'm really sorriest for is Bob Bernstein," Janey said sadly. "He was the most innocent victim of all."

"That's right; all he did was take the pictures. But that's what had the killer worried. Bob had a complete file of negatives on the original Burke Baby, and he might have started getting suspicious when he was suddenly yanked off the assignment. He was acting odd when I saw him at Sword's Point that weekend. And then there was the railroad accident—"

Janey gasped. "You really think you were pushed?"

"I'll never know for sure. But after I spent the weekend there, the killer might have thought that Bob tipped me off. That made me a potential threat. But there wasn't any doubt about the pill bottle. *That* was a definite murder attempt. I'm always leaving the damn bottle lying around my desk; it was a cinch to walk into my office when nobody was around, slip in the poison, and wait for me to say goodbye, cruel world. Fortunately, it must have been some kind of rat-poison compound that only made me sick to my stomach. But Bernstein wasn't that lucky—" Dave frowned suddenly. "You know, I still don't understand how your name got on Bob's appointment calendar. Unless the killer used your name when calling Bob—"

"That must be it," Janey sniffed. "I told everybody that Bob took wonderful portraits, just to help him out. Bob got some work out of it; he even sent me flowers, with a little thank-you note."

"Flowers? Then that's why he wrote your name in his book. And that's what the "F" meant! He was just making a note to send you a gift."

"Well, what did you *think*, for heaven's sake? That I went out there and killed him?"

"I don't know *what* I thought," Dave said foggily. "I knew the accident was more than that, that it was designed to get rid of Bob and the photographic files at the same time. But I couldn't prove that he was slugged unconscious, and that somebody deliberately started the fire. His body was too badly destroyed to give evidence—"

Janey shivered. "What a monster!"

"But Bob Bernstein wasn't to be the last victim. Because as soon as Willie Shenk agreed to write that phony blackmail letter, he was added to the must-kill list."

"But why did Willie go to the office? Why didn't he wait at the hotel?"

"Because the killer changed the appointment place, just by calling him up at the hotel and making new arrangements."

"But if Willie was helping you and Max Theringer, why didn't he tell you about the call?"

Dave grimaced. "Because Willie had a different vision. Sugarplum fairies danced in his head, all with little dollar signs on them. The only reason he agreed to the trap was to get his hands on that hundred thousand; he was planning to double-cross all the time. The call made it perfect for him. So he sneaked out the back way and went to the office, supposedly to meet your Uncle Homer and get his loot."

"But didn't the night man see them go into the building?"

"All he saw was Willie. Willie signed Homer Hagerty's name to the book and went upstairs. The killer was already there, and had been since four o'clock that afternoon—hiding in one of the washroom's de luxe suites, ducking cleaning women all night, emerging from the john only long enough to place the call to Willie and make his last appointment. Then all the killer had to do was spend the night in the office, and leave in the morning before the employees arrived to discover Willie's body. Don't you see the result? If Willie Shenk had been found on Uncle Homer's carpet, we would have *really* been convinced that he was the murderer. And the *real* killer would have gotten away."

"And Uncle Homer never showed up—"

"No, because Uncle Homer didn't have the money to pay Willie off. He found that out when he and Wilton Sheplow went to the bank, and learned that his half of the agency's capital couldn't be withdrawn without closing the agency. So he called his new partner, Grace, into the office, and told her the predicament. She refused. So instead of keeping the appointment at the hotel, Uncle Homer went home and got quietly plastered . . ."

Janey chewed her lip thoughtfully. "Money," she said. "It makes people do terrible things."

"Maybe," Dave grunted. "But the people who make the money, who work for it, sweat for it, swallow pride for it— they're not the kind who kill for it. It's the ones who *live* off money that take it most seriously. That's where the difference was. Your Uncle Homer liked money; he told me so himself. But it was a yardstick for him, a measure of his own worth in the world. Even if we had lost the Burke account, he would have loosened his button-down collar and rolled up his Brooks Brothers shirt sleeves, and made some more. The same goes for Kermit Burke. But when you look at everyone who was involved, you can see who *didn't* have that outlook, who loved money passionately but had never *earned* a cent of it."

"And there was something else," Janey said. "Plain old jealousy. Let's not forget that."

"That's right. There was a double reason for knocking off Annie Gander. Not just to protect the money that was so important, but to get rid of a rival. That's what Grace Tait was doing when she fired that gun."

Lightly, Janey touched Dave's bandaged arm.

"And to think she might have killed *you* . . ."

"I was lucky, all right. Luckier than Annie, and Bob Bernstein, and Willie, and Gordon . . ."

"Gordon?"

"That was the cruelest cut of all. When Gordon learned about Annie's murder, he got panicky and wanted to go to the police. But Grace didn't have to exert herself to get rid of Gordon. In his case, swift medication was crucial. All she had to do was . . . do nothing."

They held hands in silence for a few moments. Then Janey said:

"Dave? You're not still mad at me, are you? Because of all the fights we had?"

"Of course not."

"I was right, though, wasn't I? About Uncle Homer?"

"My favorite boss," Dave said, nibbling her fingers.

"You know how I really feel about you, Dave."

"I dunno. It's been such a long time that I forget."

Janey sneezed.

"Bless you," Dave said, getting up from the chair to sit on the edge of her bed.

Joe Spiegel walked into Dave's office, frowned at the sight of the empty chair, and stomped up to Louise's desk.

"Where's the master?" he said sourly. "He was screaming for this new Burke campaign the other day, and now I can't find him."

"Mr. Robbins won't be in," Louise said, a glint of moisture in her eyes. "He's sick."

"Sick?"

"Virus," Louise said. "Isn't it terrible how it gets around?"

About the Author

Henry Slesar has been earning his living with a typewriter since he was seventeen—turning out advertising copy for a number of agencies and currently for Fuller & Smith & Ross, where he has the impressive title of Vice-President and Creative Director. He not only likes the advertising business; he admits he likes it.

In 1955 he began to write fiction and since then has produced and sold more than 180 short stories, several of which have appeared in best-of-the-year anthologies; many have been adapted for television and one for the movies.

Mr. Slesar was born and raised in Brooklyn, now lives in an off-beat modern home in Katonah, New York, which also houses his record collection. He is an ardent jazz fan. He is married and has one child, a four-year-old daughter.